Lee

EMERSON WOLVES BOOK 5

KATHI S. BARTON

This is a work of fiction. Names, characters, places, and incidents are products of the author's imagination or are used fictitiously and are not to be construed as real. Any resemblance to actual events, locations, organizations, or persons, living or dead, is entirely coincidental.

World Castle Publishing, LLC
Pensacola, Florida
Copyright © Kathi S. Barton 2016
Paperback ISBN: 9781629894959
eBook ISBN: 9781629894966
First Edition World Castle Publishing, LLC, June 27, 2016
http://www.worldcastlepublishing.com

Licensing Notes

Cover: Karen Fuller
Editor: Eric Johnston
Editor: Maxine Bringenberg

CHAPTER 1

"He's in his cups again." Kimber only nodded. The woman standing in front of her started to tap her foot. "Well? Are you going to take over or not? Wendell has said that he'd rather die than to have to work in his place again, and Mark said that he is sick of working hard for him and getting no credit. It is up to you to take over for this evening's dinner."

"I'm only the fourth cook, not the chef by any means." Kimber knew she could do it, but it would be bad for her if she did. "He'll fire me."

"No, he won't. Who would he get to take over for him should he do this again? No one, I'm telling you. He's done this too much, and no one wants to cover for him. There are no others that can or will do this. You are all we have." Kimber glanced at the clock above Mrs. Stanton's head. "You have plenty of time, yes?"

"I'll need help. And I won't clean up after." Mrs. Stanton

looked pissed, but finally nodded. "And I want to have my own menu. Not his."

"You are going to make him upset, but I need a cook. Do what you must. But you had better be ready in time if you don't want to have to worry about him firing you."

Kimber nodded and moved to change her jacket.

As the fourth chef in a restaurant this size, and always busy, all she ever got to really do was the garnish on the plates, make the salads when they were different than the regular salad, and occasionally she'd be allowed to do the side dish. Not often, but enough for her to feel good about still working here. Kimber Gray was a first-rate cordon bleu chef and had worked in one of the most prestigious restaurants in Europe. Someday it was going to look good for her to have that on her resume when she applied to work as first chef somewhere.

At ten minutes until the dinner hour, she stepped back from her counter. The dinners would be perfect...the steaks were cut, and the fish—trout that had been earmarked for a trout almandine—had been changed to a stuffed trout with wrapped grilled asparagus, with a baby-laced Swiss sauce. Everything was as ready as she could make it. And when the first order came in, Kimber let out a long breath and began working on it.

The night wasn't really busy, but she kept on top of everything. Appetizers were inspected to make sure that they fit with what the customer was ordering. Plates were spotless when she put her food on them, and looked like works of art when they left to be served. Kimber even made sure that two of the staff had clean jackets just before they left to work.

Things were just as perfect as she could make them. After all, she wanted this to be perfect, her solo night as head chef.

She was pleased when very little came back on the plates that had been sent out, and even less of the small desserts that she'd made up when she'd realized there wasn't any to be had.

The strawberries had been fresh and the cream would have gone bad by tomorrow, so she used them both to create a lovely dessert. The fresh blueberries had been sitting in their juices since yesterday, but they were usable and she wanted some color on the plate. By the time the restaurant was ready to close, she was more than ready to go home. But the last minute order had her staying just a little longer to complete it.

The special had gone over well. And with this order, a single person had gotten the last of it. The wrapped asparagus was perfect even though it had been made up in advance, and there was leftover sauce that she put in one of the small cups and sent out with the meal. By the time the dinner was out the door, she had nothing left but a slice of cheese and a single dessert with some smashed blueberries on the side.

Pulling on her coat, she watched as the rest of the staff scrambled to clean up. As per her arrangement with Mrs. Stanton, she wasn't going to be joining them. Kimber did notice that the work station that she normally worked at wasn't even touched as yet, but it wasn't her problem. Home was awaiting her. She was so excited when she got to go back in the employee area to clock out for the night.

She was nearly home when her phone rang. "One of the last patrons would like a word with you. I think he wishes to complain."

It was Chef Hayes. His voice was slurred and he sounded very pissed. But Kimber knew that she'd done just what had been asked of her. Had he been sober, she would not have had to do his job.

"I'm sorry, but if he wishes to complain, that would be to you or to Mrs. Stanton. I'm nearly home." He started cursing and she felt her anger rise. "What is his complaint?"

"Get your skinny little ass back here and find out. And you left your station in a mess. How many times have I told you to make sure that your area is cleaned when you are finished?" He huffed. "You will never be more than a grill cook for so long as you live. Why I took you on is beyond me. And I might not have if things had been different."

"Different how? And I had an arrangement with Mrs. Stanton." He started laughing and Kimber felt the hair on her arms dance with her anger. "She said so long as I did the cooking, that others would clean my area. Also, had you not been in your cups, as she calls it, none of this would have mattered. Someone had to do your job, and I think I did a fine job of it."

"Fine job, is it? I'll say what is a fine job and not. It was shit. It's always shit when you're working. And since when is she in charge of my kitchen?" Kimber felt her own anger take on a new level when he laughed again. "You will be here in the morning first thing. I will take care of this posthaste. Do not be late, Gray, or you will rue the day that you came to think you were a chef."

She was a chef. And for the rest of her walk home in the rain, she let her tears fall. She was a chef, damn it, and she wanted to someday work in the finest restaurant as one. But there had been stumbling blocks along her journey, and she had had to work harder at her life choices. It seemed to her that for every step forward she had made, there had been four to take her back. Kimber was sick of it.

As she entered her tiny apartment, she looked at the

woman who cared for her home and daughter while she was away. Fern Blue had been with her since Hannah had been born. And now, eight years later, they were more like mother and daughter than sitter to employer. Fern had needed her as much as Kimber needed Fern, so it had worked out well for them both. She woke when Kimber opened the door to hang her coat.

"All tuckered out, she was. I had her take a lovely bath at around six and she fell asleep on my lap. We had us a good bowl of popcorn before." Kimber nodded and sent Fern to her room. Going to her daughter's room, she paused in the doorway to watch her. Kimber would bet anything that Hannah had been up since she'd been in this room.

"What are you doing up so late, young lady?" Hannah turned and grinned at her, the book she'd been reading still in her hands. "What is it you're reading now?"

"*Moby Dick.*" Kimber moved into her daughter's room and looked at the worn book. "Mr. Fillmore gave it to me. He said it was a classic. I think Mr. Fillmore is a classic."

"I'm sure he is too. But you should be sleeping. Don't you have school tomorrow?" Hannah nodded and wrapped her body around Kimber's when she picked her up. "You're almost too heavy for me to carry anymore. When will you be carrying me?"

Hannah laughed as she put her in bed. As her daughter closed her eyes, sleep taking her almost immediately, Kimber looked around the room. She felt tears fill her eyes when she thought of all the ways she'd failed her only child.

The furniture in the room was second hand. Some of it was third or fourth hand, even. Her clothing was all things that she'd picked up here and there...a friend's child had outgrown them, a tag sale that she'd found out about. Her books were new. Not the writers that her daughter adored, but her work books and other subject books for her classes, and the extra classes that she'd been taking.

Hannah was brilliant, read well beyond her years, and was a whiz at math. While her age had her listed as a third grader, the teachers at her school had been giving her work well beyond her grade level for months now, and it had improved Hannah's wellbeing by not being bored in her classroom.

Dozing slightly, Kimber got up and went to the kitchen. There was just enough food in the cupboards to last until her next check. Instead of eating anything, Kimber made herself a cup of tea, her only luxury, and sat down to drink it. Something was going to happen tomorrow, and Kimber knew that with her luck, it wouldn't be good.

~~~

Lee watched as the women worked the line. He'd arrived early this morning, just as the sun was coming up, and he wanted to make sure that everything he'd put in place before he left was where it should be. Then he was going to take a long, well-deserved nap. For about three days, if he was lucky.

The smack to the back of his head had him turning to his father.

"You should have called when you were coming in. Someone would have picked you up at the airport. Now we have to figure out how to have a welcome home party on such short notice." Lee hugged his dad and told him he loved him. "I love you too, boy. But you should have called. What are you doing here this early?"

"I wanted to make sure that Dawn's lines were working well before she went into production next week." The two of them watched the line of women, three at the first part of the line and two more at each station after. The line, nothing more than a long set of burners that had been strung together, was going to make it so that Dawn could make ten to twelve batches of jams and jellies at each place, rather than just three or four as she'd been doing at her single stove. When he was satisfied that the work table was close enough to the stove so as not to be a bother, he moved to the other part of the building. His dad asked him if he'd gotten things set up for Sloan.

"Yes. I made sure she had good people in the kitchen and that they know what she wants done each day. I think that if I ever open my own business, I'm going to make sure that there is a kitchen with staff on duty like she has. It's a nice place to eat. The food is healthy without being stale, and it's a great place for them to go and relax. I do think that she's going to need to expand in a few years, but she said that would be something that she'd have to look into. I think she said she was landlocked."

"Yeah, I heard her telling Hunter that when the time was right, she'd have to go over there and see to it. I'm thinking that they might be making a trip when that baby is here. She's looking ready to pop." Lee nodded. He knew that Sloan only had a month to go, and he was excited about holding his niece soon. "You hear about the little one that Luke and Jack got? He's a pistol, all right. And he's looking forward to having a fishing day with me soon. Mike and his boy have come down and they showed us what we need. When you gonna make me a granddaddy?"

"I'm thinking that I should find a mate first, don't you?" His dad snorted at him. "I've been sort of busy. And so you know, I'm not in all that big of a hurry to find her right now.

11

I have a house, but it's being worked on. I have a job, but I'm all over the world trying to make it work, and in the event that you didn't notice, I'm working more than I am socializing."

"Yeah, I've seen that too. What do I have to do, go out and find her for you like I did the rest of them?" Lee just lifted his brow at his dad. "You know that I had to get Sloan and Hunter together. Luke would still be dangling at the end of his sticks had I not charmed my way into Jack's heart first. And then there is Ellis and Jarrett. I'm about worn out keeping the women coming in just to find your mates for you all."

"I think you should just let the women find us. Graham has finished school, but he's got things going on, and I have to find my own niche in life before I can even think of settling down." Lee thought of his brother Graham. "Has he...you know, has he moved on yet?"

"Not that I can see. Finding that body nearly done him in. I know that the police never thought he'd done it, but I think he still has him a few dreams about it. Can you imagine working on a log jam and finding a woman all wrapped up in them limbs? She'd been there for some time, too, those people said." His dad watched the line as it moved in the right direction. "You thinking that he'll stay holed up in that house of his for the next fifty years?"

"I don't know, Dad. When I talked to him last week, he told me that he's doing fine, but he sounded like he wasn't. I'm going to try and see him while I'm here. Sloan said that his house is coming along well." His dad nodded. "But as for my mate, I think I can wait her out, don't you?"

"You mean wait until she falls in your lap before you figure out she's the best thing that could have happened to you." Lee had changed the subject on purpose, just to bring his

12

dad around from thinking about it too much. His dad seemed to have gotten the hint for now, and asked about what he was looking at now in Dawn's building.

"Jack told Dawn that she'd save big bucks if she printed her own labels. Jarrett set her up with the right kind of printer and the perfect paper, and all Dawn has to do is make what she needs. This will save her from having tons of inventory around just waiting to be used. Jack also told her that if she wanted to add something to them, like sugar-free if she went that far, then it would be easy to print up a few labels instead of a million or so that might not work out." The machines were still now, the labels having been printed up a few days ago, but he liked the way it had been streamlined to not take up too much of her upper level. "I didn't have anything to do with this part, but I can see that they had Jarrett up here. It's nice."

As they made their way around the large building, Lee noticed that the kitchen area that he'd suggested be set up was well underway. Sandwiches were in the coolers right now, but he knew that in a few days, when people started to show up to work, there would be hot food as well as some cold for the employees. All of it was a perk to working here. He had also suggested to Dawn that she open a little shop one day and have some of her jams for sale in it, along with her scones and breads.

His dad moved to the large desk at the front of the building when they were nearly finished with their self-guided tour. Martha Brooks was running the phones today. Lee had heard from Hunter that Mary Peacock and Claribel Sharp had been taking turns working the desk for Dawn. The women had come from Hunter's pack, but he knew that they loved working for his brother and his wife.

He was startled when the phone call that had just come in was for him.

"I just found out that you're in town." He could hear the hurt in Sloan's voice. "You go and see your brother before me? How could you?"

"I haven't seen Ellis or Dawn at all since I got here. I thought they were down there." She told him she didn't know anything anymore. "I'm sorry, honey. I just got in a few hours ago and had the plane bring me here instead of home so that I wouldn't have to worry about this the entire time I'm home with you guys."

"Good save." He laughed with her. "I'm just bored, if you want to know the truth. Your dad and I have put in as much garden as we dare already, but I want to get out there and dig the places up for my tomatoes. Did your dad tell you that we have first leaves already? They're beautiful."

"No. He's been hounding me about a grandbaby." His dad popped him in the back of the head. "And he's abusing me too. I tell you, I'd be better off just staying away sometimes."

"Oh no, don't do that. What would I do without my family around me?" He didn't answer her but smiled. "I've been thinking about some things that I'd like for you to look into. I have this place here in town that I want to convert into something...I don't know, bigger. Like a steakhouse, but not."

"You mean something more than the diner in your town, and with bigger ticket items." She told him that was about right. "I ate a late dinner last night at this place where I was staying called simply *Parfaitement Fait,* or Perfectly Made in English. I had a stuffed trout that was so good I tried to go back and hire the chef. They told me that the chef had gone for the night, and all I got for my troubles was some drunk blowing his drunk-assed breath on me."

Her laughter made him smile. "And what would you have hired him for? You're not thinking of being my competition, are you? I'm hoping so. Because I have to tell you that sounds delicious. Actually, everything sounds good to me. I'm always starved."

"You're eating for two, so small wonder. And no, I'm not going to be competing with you in anything. I like to keep my own little corner of this world pissed off Sloan free. And the guy I talked to last night, I had a feeling...well, he didn't strike me as the one who had made the meal. There was something...I don't know. I knew that he was lying and he had no idea what I was talking about. He said I was to have had trout almandine and that I had it wrong. Like I said, he smelled of liquor too."

"Let me make a few phone calls. I know the restaurant. I don't know what I can do, but I can find out for you. Perhaps we can persuade him to come here and open our venture." Lee said nothing. He had thought when he went to school that he wanted to be this great cook. And now that he'd been working for Sloan and Hunter, he'd discovered that while he loved to cook, he was more into making the place work than being the chef. He enjoyed what he did more than anything he'd ever done before. Being a food critic for some really important newspapers was a dream he'd never even considered, but he loved it as much as he did figuring out problems at some really nice restaurants.

"Just let me know. Dad and I will be there by tonight. I'm telling you now so you won't be disappointed that I will be there for dinner, but I need to go to bed. I think I've been up for three days straight." She told him that they'd expect him for dinner, and that maybe Ellis and Dawn could make it back as well, and that he should ask them. "I'll see what I can do."

After hanging up, he told Dad what they'd talked about as they made their way to Ellis's house. The building that Dawn was in was close to the house, so they opted to walk. As soon as they were in the yard, Lee stood back and stared.

"Yeah, nice, huh?" He glanced over at Ellis as he came out of the barn just behind him. His brother looked very relaxed and happy as he continued. "We weren't sure that we wanted it this big, but the more we thought about it, the bigger the house got. There's room if you want to stay tonight. I know that Dawn would love it."

"Sloan and the rest of them are expecting all of us for dinner." Ellis nodded and took him to the house. "Christ, this is gorgeous. What the hell? Did you win the lottery?"

"No. We ran into some unexpected money." Lee nodded. He'd heard about the inheritance from Dawn's family, and that they had accepted her into their family with open arms. "When we showed them the house we were building before we left for our honeymoon, they were happy. But when we got back, there were more rooms on the framing, as well as a whole upper level that we'd had no idea about. Her grandparents said that when they come to visit they want to burden us with their presence."

Lee laughed and so did Ellis. He was taking them in the front of the house just as Dawn came from the back of it. He hugged her tightly, ignoring the growls coming from Ellis. Dawn looked wonderfully happy too.

"You'll stay for dinner?" He told her what he'd told Ellis. "Oh. I guess we should go. The family has been excited for you to come home for weeks now. I'm so glad that you've made it home safely. How long will you be here?"

"I'm hoping a couple of months. I have some projects here that I can take care of, and two on the burner for Sloan. But I'm hoping everything can be worked on from here." She asked him about his house. "I'm hoping to get it done too. Mostly it's just moving stuff in that I've already ordered. There are some decisions that I need to make. Most of them are things that I could probably have taken care of over the phone, but I wanted to be there too. I miss you guys."

"We missed you too. I guess you've been to the plant?" He nodded. "I'm so nervous. Not about the lines that you helped me get set up, but all of it. I'm so worried that I won't be very good at this."

Ellis laughed before talking. "Yeah, those nearly two million dollars in orders mean that she's going to fail big time. I mean, who would want to buy her things anyway?"

"You have that much in pre-orders?" Ellis told him that was just on her website. She had nearly double that for stores wanting to carry her line. "Holy shit, Dawn, that's wonderful. I'm very proud of you."

"I'm nearly sick with it." Lee looked at Ellis over her head when he hugged her again. He mouthed the word *Basil* and he nodded.

Her uncle, a man by the name of Basil Combs, had been found criminally insane by the courts. Other charges were pending: kidnapping, murder, as well as abuse to a corpse. But those were on the back burner until they could figure out the names of all the women, some dead and others still coming forward, that had in some way been harmed by the man. Basil's mother had been murdered as well, and they were still trying to pin that on his list. The man had been taking women or children from their homes for decades. His "wife," Neva, had been one of many that had been brought into the house as a play-thing, and had ended up living out the rest of her life with him. He'd also kidnapped Dawn's mother, and had made her daughter's life a living hell when she'd told him off. Life, as far as Lee could see it, was a never-ending line of people shitting on one another to get to where they wanted. Thank goodness his family wasn't like that.

As they boarded the plane a few hours later, Lee was dozing in the seat when his dad touched his arm. He had to stare at him for several seconds before he realized that he was talking to him about the phone.

"You okay, son?" He nodded and took the phone from his dad. "You look like you've not slept in about a month. You sure you should be going to dinner tonight?"

"Yeah, I'm fine. Just really tired." He put the phone to his ear just as the pilot was telling them they were ten minutes from landing. Lee said his name in the phone as he started to pull on his seat buckle.

"Mr. Emerson? Is this Lee Emerson, the food critic? I've heard so many things about you." Lee told him that he was in flight, and that he needed him to tell him why he'd called. "Sir, there is a problem with the request that I have in for Mrs. Emerson. She called my restaurant just today requesting the information on the chef that had cooked the night you were there. I'm sorry, sir, but the chef said that the person you were asking for is no longer with the restaurant."

"I see. Can you tell me why?" He said that he wasn't sure. That as the owner of the restaurant, he had given full control over the kitchen to his chef. "And so you have no idea that the man you left in charge was drunk when I saw him just before leaving? Nor that the meal that I had that night was one of the best that I've ever eaten?"

"Drunk? Oh no, sir. That couldn't have been our chef. He no longer drinks." Lee looked at Ellis when he touched his arm. They were at the airport, but he wanted him to take his time with the call. "He said that when he spoke to you, you were confused about the food that you were served. Are you sure you had the right restaurant?"

"I'm sure. And you can be sure of this...if he fired this person that cooked for me, then you have made the stupidest decision you have ever made when it comes to running a restaurant. And I'm going to write up an article on it and say that, too. Not only did the staff look relaxed and happy, but the food, all of it, was outstanding. I noticed that when I was speaking to him that the entire kitchen staff looked like they were ready for him to explode. And he did, twice, while I was there."

"I assure you, sir, that I've never heard of anything like this from this restaurant. You can be assured that I will look into this. There are some...well, I won't bore you with the details, but I've noticed some issues on the paperwork on that particular place. I'll take care of it." Lee told him he'd better if he wanted to remain in business for long. "If I do find that you are correct, I will get back with you."

"You do that. But I have a feeling that the next time I talk to you, you're going to be telling me that you're going out of business and that it was all because of the chef you have now. If I were you, and you know my reputation if you've heard my name, I'd be looking into the chef you have now and start asking questions. You're about to get a rude awakening."

Lee

CHAPTER 2

Kimber sat in her apartment and thought about what had happened just a few short hours ago. She'd not just been fired, but she'd also had her name placed on the list. The list that would prevent her from getting any kind of restaurant job in this country. Kimber knew that she'd not even get a job washing dishes now. She looked up when Fern said her name.

"What are you going to do, dear?" Kimber told her she had no idea. "Poor thing. You can't seem to get a break, now can you? What will you do for money? I don't have any, but if I did, you'd be welcome to it."

"I know that. I'm sorry about this." Fern waved her off. "I'm glad that Hannah isn't here to see me like this. I feel like such a failure."

"No, you're not. You just trusted those people to have your back. I bet that he had them say those things so that you'd look bad." Which was true. "And those people are going to be sorry for firing you too. You was the best there was. But don't you worry none about me. I can go and live with my daughter and her brood. They've been wanting me there anyways."

"I've called my aunt. She's...she's not a nice person, but I have to have some help. I guess we'll have to stay with her for a few weeks. Just until I can find us a place to live." Fern nodded and told her that family was good to have around when stuff like this happened. "Yes. I suppose it is."

Only Great Aunt Kimberly wasn't one that you would normally depend on when things were bad. She wasn't even sure that anyone would want to go to her when things were going well. She was, far and away, the coldest woman that Kimber knew. Also the meanest. And asking her for help had been harder than she'd thought it would have been.

After Fern left, her meager belongings all packed up, Kimber started looking around for things that she could sell. There was no point in waiting to be evicted, so she'd talked to Fern immediately and had set up with her landlord that she was going to have to go soon. Since she wasn't going to be able to return, not with the cost of things and her situation, she couldn't put her things in storage. Not to mention, she'd never be able to afford the rent on a storage facility.

She was putting together a handwritten flyer when her little girl came home. Hannah had lived in France her entire life. Kimber was from the US and was only here because of her schooling. It had been her mom's last wish, sort of, to have Kimber come here and do what she wanted to do no matter what. Kimber had worked very hard to do the best she could, and had still failed her.

Her daughter had citizenship in both countries until she was eighteen because of her birth situation. But right now, all Kimber could think about was how she had failed her daughter in two countries.

"Will we have a house?" Kimber told her that she was going to work on that. "But we might have a yard, right? Somewhere I can play if I want to?"

"Yes. I'll make sure that we have some yard. I'm not sure how much." Hannah nodded, but she still looked unsure. "I'm waiting for my great aunt to call me back. If we could stay with her for a little while, we can save up our money and maybe buy us a little house somewhere. Somewhere there are children your age."

"I guess we'll have to sell our stuff, too. We can't take it with us." Kimber told her no, but she could take a few things. "I don't have much anyway. Not that it matters...I can only play with one thing at a time."

Kimber felt her heart twist in her chest at her little girl's words. She'd tried so hard to make it better for her and had failed so badly. So many things, nearly from the very beginning of her finding out that she was pregnant with her, had gone wrong.

"I've got someone to buy the couch and chair that we have. I think there might be enough money after we get the tickets to get one of those reader things for you." Hannah brightened, then shook her head. "I can swing it, Hannah. And I want you to have it. We're going to be broke for a while after we get to the United States, and it might be the last time I can get you something really nice for a while."

"I love you, Mommy." Kimber held her daughter while she cried. They both were crying when the phone rang, and when she reached for it, she nearly hung up again when she heard her great aunt's voice.

"So, you're coming home with your tail between your legs, are you? Failed, just like I said you would, didn't you? Well, I'm hoping that you know that every day I'm going to be telling you that." Kimber nodded to the phone, too hurt to answer her. "And I'm supposing that brat of yours will be living here too. What am I supposed to do with a child running around breaking my things?"

"She's very well behaved. And I'll replace anything she might break." Her aunt asked her how she was going to do that. "I don't know. But I'll make sure you're paid back for all of this."

"I never said I'd take you in yet. I have to think on it. Do you have any idea how much this is going to cost me?" Kimber said nothing. Her aunt was the richest person she knew and had more money than Midas, her mom used to say. But she was as tight as a virgin on her wedding night. "When do you thinking of scurrying home? Soon, if you've been fired from that restaurant. I told you that wouldn't work out, didn't I?"

"Yes, ma'am, you did." It was on the tip of her tongue to tell her she was always right because she made sure she was, but said nothing else. What would be the point? And she needed her to help her, even for a little while. The silence at the other end of the phone did nothing to help her nerves.

Kimber had no idea what she'd do if she turned them down. They'd be living on the street if she did. Kimber didn't even have a car that they could live in. When Hannah got up and moved to her room, Kimber leaned her head back on the couch. One thing she'd learned in dealing with her aunt was to not rush her. It would do Kimber little good, and it would just piss her aunt off more.

"I'm guessing you don't have a pot to piss in, do you,

Kimber? Not even the plane fare to come and sponge off me and my money." Kimber wanted to tell her that she'd have it, but didn't know if she would. She and Hannah only had five days left on their lease for the month. "Answer me, girl, when I talk to you."

"I don't have it." She listened to her aunt go on about rainy days and saving for it. Then she went on to ask about the brat of a daughter and if her father was going to take her. "Hannah's father is dead. I've told you that before. He didn't even know about her."

"Should have, don't you think? When you have sex, you should expect there to be an issue. Have you never heard of precautions? Don't they have that sort of thing there?" She told her that they did. "Oh, so you wanted to find yourself in a family way, did you? Never thinking, I've told you that all your life. Your mother was the same way. Her head in the clouds and never thinking of the consequences."

Hannah came out of her room again. She had her bank and a small mallet that had been in the kitchen. When she sat before her, Kimber started to cry harder, hard enough that her aunt could hear her this time.

"Stop that blubbering right now." Kimber tried, but it was difficult. "I'll expect you to pay me back, with interest, for this. There are no free rides, not even for you. And rent. You'll pay me rent each and every week until you have enough to get out on your own. Where you should have been all along."

"I'll sign a contract if you wish." Her aunt laughed and said that was a sure thing. "I don't have long here. Only a few days."

"There are tickets for you at the airport already. You have to be out on the seven-thirty flight day after tomorrow." She asked her if she meant her time zone or hers. "Mine. Why do I care what your time is? Don't make me have to pay fines because you couldn't get yourself ready in time. And there will be money delivered to you sometime tomorrow. I'm assuming that you'll be there since you've been fired from your job. Make sure that you're dressed befitting of my family. I will not have you coming here in those rags you wear."

After she hung up, two things occurred to Kimber. First of all, her aunt had taken care of things before she'd called her back, and second, that she'd been keeping an eye on her. And even though it sounded like she cared, Kimber knew it was because she would want to know when she was failing.

Hannah asked her if she'd break her bank for her.

"All right, but only because we won't be able to take it in the luggage." Hannah nodded and Kimber brought the little hammer down on the bank. There were a few dollars in it, but mostly change, and all of it would have to be exchanged before they left here. "That's your money, Hannah. And as soon as Mrs. Fitzpatrick pays me for our furniture, we'll go and get dinner. We should celebrate one time before we leave."

Mrs. Fitzpatrick had bought not only her living room things, but her bed, as well as the dressers that she'd had to dump on the floor. By the time her son came to get the things, Hannah had packed most of the things she was going to take. The fifty-three dollars that she'd had in her bank was sealed up in a zip bag and deep in the pockets of her suitcase. It was a pitiful amount of things that they were both going to be leaving with.

After they had their dinner of burgers and fries, Hannah had gone to bed and Kimber lay out on the floor beside her. She had several million things running through her head, and a list that was growing longer with each beat of her heart. Along with getting to the airport, she had to contact Hannah's school and make arrangements to get her transcripts, and she also had to get her daughter's medical records, along with her own. Then there was the bills that she was going to owe, small things, but she'd have to make arrangements for them to be paid and get Hannah the reader. There was enough to buy it, but little left over for much in the way of food for their trip. Kimber fell into a fitful sleep when the sun was coming up again.

~~~

Lee opened his eyes and smiled. He was home. And he was going to stay here for a while, too. After talking to Sloan and Hunter, he told them that he just needed to relax for a little while. A month if possible.

"I think you should stay for as long as you want. The baby will be coming soon, and I'd really like to have you here." Lee had thought that a good idea too and told Hunter that. "And I heard about your restaurant that you're opening."

He had only glanced at Sloan and she laughed. He wasn't ready to even talk about that just yet. But when Lee went up to bed, his house just too far to navigate to, Sloan told him that she had a building in mind. Lee had started to tell her that he didn't want it, but she only patted him on the cheek.

"It's not anywhere near being ready to use. There is some work to be done, but I'm going to have it done with the idea that it's going to be a nice place." He nodded. "Maybe I'll have found your chef by then, and you and he can run it."

He had gone to bed thinking that if anyone could find him, it would be her. And that was the last thing he'd thought of all night. Getting up, he made his way to the shower and then down to eat some lunch. He'd not realized it had been so late. And he found out that it was later than even that when his dad told him he'd been asleep for two and a half days.

"You must have been right up there with exhausted." Lee nodded, his mind still trying to wrap around the fact that he'd slept so long. "You got plans? I'm about to head myself over to the diner and see Mabel. She's got herself some new recipes that she wants me to try out for her. And some fine apple pie that Dawn baked for her. I'm telling you, a man could die content with daughters as good to me as mine are."

"I'm going to head over to the house. I need to make some decisions about some stuff. Carpet and things." His dad nodded and moved out of the house just as Lee's cell phone rang. Answering it, he knew that whoever was on the other line was going to be disappointed if they wanted him to do anything today.

"Mr. Emerson?" He said it was. "This is Margo Stanton. You spoke to the owner of *Parfaitement Fait* the other day. I might have some information on the chef you were looking for."

"I'm sorry, Ms. Stanton, but I'm no longer in France. I do hope that the owner has had a change of heart and taken the chef back." When she started crying, all Lee could think about was why now. "I assure you that if he doesn't, it matters little to me."

"He was drunk. And I lied for him. We all did." Lee frowned, not sure what she meant, and he told her that. "He told me that if I didn't tell the owner that he was sober and that he'd cooked your meal, I'd be out as quickly as Kimber was. I need my job, Mr. Emerson. So me and three other people lied to keep ours...and now it seems that we're all going to be out of work. The real owner, a person from the United States, is closing us down, telling us they no longer need us open."

"Perhaps it would be best if you told me what you're talking about. I'm sorry, but what does this have to do with me, and who did you lie about? And while you're at it, who is Kimber?" The woman cried harder and Lee closed his eyes. He wasn't sure what was going on, but he really didn't want to have to fuck with this too. "What do you mean, you're all going to be out of work?"

"The restaurant, it's being closed down as of day after tomorrow. Some of us think it's because of what happened with Kimber, but now we're not so sure. Word has gotten around about the review that was posted, and how someone had said on one of those social pages that the place had gone to hell. Will you post a retraction so we can stay open?" Sloan came into the kitchen with him and he told her what was going on. Or as much as he knew was going on. He asked for a computer, and she told him there was one in Hunter's office he could use. It took him nearly ten minutes of the woman crying to figure out what she was talking about.

"You see it?" He told her that he was reading it now and that he'd not written it. "It happened again after Kimber was fired, him being too drunk to make any kind of sense of what he was saying to us. I thought that if he was sober enough to stand up and yell at the staff then he could surely cook. But I guess I was wrong. And with this review, business dropped off to nearly nothing. Last night we had open tables all night long. And we always had a waiting list."

"So this Chef Hayes made dinner for this other critic and it wasn't up to par. Invite him back. Have him tell the man he was having a bad night, that he'd just fired someone and the kitchen was getting their feet under them. This other person, Kimber…how does he fit into this?"

The article had not mentioned the name, so he assumed that either the man was a lower cook or was off. Mrs. Stanton sobbed harder as she told him who Kimber was.

"Kimber Gray was the woman who cooked your dinner that night you were there. We all knew it was her, and that was who we lied about for her to be fired. I told her that I'd make sure that everyone knew she'd done it because of Hayes being in his cups, but I didn't. I…he threatened me and now… now we're out of work too." Lee looked up when Sloan came into the room with him. He wanted to tell her to stay put. Her body looked ready to explode, but as she had every time someone asked her, she told them she had never felt better.

"I'm still sort of confused why you're calling me. I mean, it was a fantastic meal, one of the best I'd had in a while. I tried to tell the owner that he should keep him…her on staff, but he seemed to think that I had lost my mind. Other than that, I'm not sure what you think I can do about your plight."

"Can you find her for us? If you can't retract the review, then can you find her so we can try and stay open?" He asked how he was supposed to do that. "She's there in the United States. I don't know when she left here, but her apartment is empty of her things and there is no forwarding address that I can find. I want to…I need to tell her how sorry I am for what I did and see if she'll come back."

Lee scrubbed his hand over his face. "Do you have any idea how big the United States is? Do you at least know what state she's in? I don't know if I can help you, but that would narrow it down." She told him she had no idea. His wolf stirred along his skin then, and he wondered what had him so upset. Then he looked at the woman standing in the doorway and stood up. "I have to call you back.

Lee was always nervous around Lady Clementine Mantle, less so when her granddaughter was around to act as a buffer. But Addie was working on a project, he'd been told, and hadn't been able to get away. Lady Mantle came into the room and sat on the couch next to Sloan.

"Hello, my dear. How are you and that lovely baby doing? I should think you are ready to have it." Sloan laughed and told her not just yet. "Well, I'm here now so that I can be here for the event. And to see my estates. Did you know that Addie has hired two more people to work for her? Her business is growing well."

"It is. But I'm pretty sure you didn't come here to talk to me about Addie. I'm assuming you need Lee." Lady Mantle nodded and pinned him with her gaze. "Well, I'll leave you to it. I have some things to set out for Cash to plant next week."

Lee wanted to beg her not to leave him, but when the door shut behind Sloan, he knew this was going to be bad. He looked at Lady Mantle and tried to think what to say to her.

It wasn't as if she had ever been mean to him. Or for that matter, he'd never done anything to piss her off. But she intimidated him to no end. And his wolf too. When she leaned back in her seat, Lee sat up straighter in his.

"I need something from you." He told her anything. "Don't be too hasty. It's not a small thing that I ask you. It involves a woman that I loathe and her grandniece."

"I'm not going to date her." Lady Mantle laughed. "I'm sorry. That came out very wrong. But I don't enjoy being set up, because it usually turns out badly for both of us."

"I'm not that devious; and besides, you're much too

handsome to need someone like me to set you up. No, this is about the grandniece, as I was saying. She's coming here soon to live with her aunt, and I don't want her to feel...I should explain something first. Kimberly Schroeder, have you heard of her? She lives on the other side of town from here."

"The older lady that walks around thinking that her money is too good to part with?" Lady Mantle laughed and Lee flushed. "You bring out the worst in me. I'm not sure why, but I feel like a babbling idiot whenever you're around me."

"Why is that?" He told her he had no idea and she smiled at him. "I like you, Lee. Very much. Your father did a good job raising you, as did your mother, but I think you've learned a great deal on your own. And I'm betting that there is a great deal that your family does not know about."

He said nothing, thinking it was the best way to deal with this. Lee also knew that, like her granddaughter, she could read his mind and his thoughts without much effort. Sometimes it was creepy the way that Addie could tell what was going to happen long before it did. He looked at Lady Mantel when something occurred to him.

"This woman, this grandniece, is she my mate? Are you setting this up so that I meet her and we live happily ever after? Because if you think that's what is going to happen, then you should know that I've no desire to meet a woman this way. Fate might be showing you her hand, but I don't need to know it." Lady Mantle only smiled. "I'm not sure I like that anymore than when Addie does it."

"I have never met the girl, to be honest with you. I just know that she's on her way here, and when she does arrive, it's going to go badly for her for a time." He nodded and asked her what she needed for him to do. "I would like for you to make sure that if she needs someone, I can depend on you to…to help her. As you may have noticed, Kimberly is not the nicest person in the world."

"No, she's not. But what sort of help do you think I can offer her? And let's stop beating around the bush, please? I have enough on my plate at the moment." When she nodded at him, he felt like a butterfly pinned to the wall. He nearly told her he'd changed his mind about helping her, but she spoke first.

"Her name is Kimber Gray. And she's a chef that is out of work."

Lee felt himself nodding, and he might have even said something, but the next thing he knew, his brother was yelling at him to breathe and Sloan was crying. When he stood up, it was all he could do not to run and never come back.

CHAPTER 3

The limo driver just stared at her. She had a feeling that her aunt had told him not to help her in any way. She was fine with that. Kimber decided that she was home now, and that if her aunt was going to play games, she could as well. Hannah pulled on her sleeve and she looked down at her.

"I'm hungry and I have to go to the bathroom." Nodding, Kimber asked the lady at the outside desk if there was a ladies' room close. Nodding as the lady pointed her in the right direction, Kimber lifted up her two bags and her daughter's one and headed in that direction. The driver opened the door to the long sleek machine but didn't bother helping her. Going by him, Kimber felt like she had won this battle, small as it was.

Kimber used the bathroom as well, and waited for Hannah to finish while she looked in the mirror. Traveling had never been something she enjoyed. She supposed it had to do with how broke she'd been, which would sour anyone on it. But the coach seating and the three plane changes had taken their toll on her, and her daughter too. When she came out of the stall, Kimber went to Hannah to help her with her clothing.

"I'm hungry now." She told her that she was as well. "Do you think we can have something before we go to that woman's house? I'll pay this time."

"Oh, darling." Kimber tried to stop the tears, but she was exhausted and humiliated. Her aunt had promised her money to be delivered. *How far did she think seventy-five dollars would go*, Kimber wondered, not for the first time. "I think I can swing a burger for us and a drink. We'll have to share."

"Okay." Oh, to be eight and able to bounce back from everything so quickly. "That man out there, with the big car, is that for us? I've never ridden in one of those before. Do you think he'll let me stick my head out the window on the top?"

"No, and don't ask him. I have a feeling that he will report us for an infraction."

Hannah giggled. As they bypassed the man with the open door, she wondered if she'd ever be this carefree again. Hannah sat on one of the tall chairs that were in front of the pretty little cart, and asked if she could have a burger with nothing on it.

"Not even cheese?" The lady behind the little counter just smiled at her. Kimber thought that she had the kindest smile for some reason. "I might even have some pickles around here too, if you want those."

"No thank you, we're on a tight budget." Kimber felt her face heat up and nearly told Hannah to hush, but the woman laughed.

"Yeah, me too. I can never stick to it when it comes to

pickles, however. But the pickles, like the cheese, are free today." Kimber frowned at the woman when she looked at her before continuing. "We're having a buy a burger with cheese and get one for free special."

"You don't have to do that." The woman only laughed and turned her back to them to put four burgers on the grill. The man that had been at the car came to the stand and cleared his throat.

"Miss, you and the young miss are to come with me. Mrs. Schroeder is waiting for you." The woman at the grill turned to them and looked at the man. "You are to stay out of this. You have been warned before."

"Don't you dare threaten her." Kimber felt her anger hit an all new level. "You tell her you're sorry right this minute, or I'll tell my aunt what kind of people she has working for her."

He only laughed at her and walked away. When he got into the car and drove away, Kimber thought for sure that she and Hannah were going to be out on the streets in very short order.

In no time they each had a double cheeseburger with fries, and bottles of water as well. Kimber was no longer hungry, fear of what she might have just done to them weighing heavy on her mind.

"You have to eat. You can't take her on if you're weak from hunger." Kimber nodded at the woman. "I'm Mabel Carlyle. You are related to the dragon, I'm guessing."

When Hannah laughed, the woman turned to her and pinched her cheek, warning her that she shouldn't call her great aunt that to her face. Kimber had a feeling that she should have held her tongue about her aunt a few times over the last couple of days too.

"She's my great aunt. Hannah and I are going to be staying with her for a few months." Kimber looked to where the limo had been. "At least I thought so. I'm not sure now. I don't think...she's not happy with us being here. And to be honest, I'm not so thrilled about being here either."

"No, I don't think that woman has been happy a day in her life. But perhaps this little one could bring a smile to her face." Kimber thought that her aunt's face would break should she ever smile, but said nothing to Mabel. "You looking for work?"

"I am. I don't know if there is much around here, but I can cook." Mabel nodded and handed Hannah another order of fries. Kimber looked down at her plate and wondered when she'd eaten her food.

"You're a little stressed out, I can see that. But if you can cook, I might have you some work. I own the local diner. My cook has just got it in his head that he wants to go to California." She made that sound like he'd said he was moving to another planet. "You come on by once you get the two of you settled and we'll talk."

Kimber felt better until she pulled out her phone to call a cab. If there even was one in this little town. She'd forgotten to turn the phone back on after the plane had landed, and now she was sure she was in deep shit. There were five messages on it, and she knew who they were from. Her aunt was the only one with this number, and she'd made good use, no doubt, of the voice mail on it.

They got progressively meaner as she listened. By the time the car pulled up in front of her and Hannah, Kimber was so upset that when the man stood there not helping them again, she walked up to him and slapped him across the face. Enough was enough.

His low growl only made her more pissed. "You told her that I was fucking some man on the couch? You actually told her that I had offered myself to you in exchange for money? What kind of person are you?"

"Employed." When she drew back to hit him again, he grabbed her arm and pulled it up behind her back. "You ever touch me again and I will make not just your stay here a nightmare, but that of your child too. Who do you think she'd believe if you told her that I'd taken your daughter to my bed?"

Kimber was suddenly free and the man that held her was gone. In his place was a large snarling wolf that looked like he would have her for dinner. But he was nothing compared to the one that stood in front of him. Mabel grabbed her by the shoulder and pulled her out of the way. Hannah was in the little food cart behind the counter when Mabel shoved her inside. Kimber watched the two wolves circle one another, knowing that when one attacked, the limo driver was going to be dead.

"Who is he?" Mabel just looked at her. "The bigger wolf? I'm assuming that he's the alpha around here."

"He is. I called Hunter when I realized what was going on and what that man had done to you the first time he rolled off without you. I didn't know you were related to the dragon, but after he left you, I figured you were no more welcome there than I would be." Kimber only nodded. "You know a wolf somewhere?"

"I did...we did. He's...he was killed." She glanced down at Hannah, who had pulled her headphones out of her pack and was watching something on her reader. She knew that the little girl was trying to drown out the violence. It was something she had done when the neighbors in their apartment building fought. They were the wolves. "Hannah saw them fighting and they changed. When they would fight they'd…it would spill over into the hall. One night the woman shot the man while Hannah was there. I'm not sure how much she saw, but when the woman turned the gun on herself too, the police never knew she'd seen anything. Hannah said he'd been the wolf before she shot him, and when he lay there, he'd changed. The woman told Hannah to go inside, and that was when she killed herself."

"The pack would have torn her up." The loud crash had her looking at the two wolves. The bigger wolf — Hunter, she supposed his name was — had the driver down on the ground and his teeth at his throat. "You should know that Hunter is a good man. He'd never do anything to hurt you."

"Everyone hurts you in the end." Mabel said nothing, and Kimber sat on the floor and held her daughter. "I have no idea why I trust you so much. I feel as if I have known you for my whole life."

"I'm a wolf. Did you know that?" Kimber shook her head. "More than ever now, the dragon is going to make it hell on you, won't she?"

"I'm betting that we're homeless again." Kimber looked up at her when she heard the scream of pain from one of the men. "I have to pay her back for bringing us here. I don't have it, and I don't know how long it will take me to get it. But she was going to charge me rent for living with her. And she's not at all happy about my daughter being here too."

"Like I said before, you have any trouble, come find me.

I'll help you best I can." Kimber nodded and held Hannah. When Mabel told her it was over, whatever that meant, Kimber gathered up her things and got into the truck with a man named Dan. He said he'd take her to her aunt's. There was blood on the ground near where the two wolves had been, but nothing more. Both of them, the two wolves, were gone.

~~~

Lee listened to his brothers go on about this and that. His head was pounding and he just wanted them to go home. He didn't want to be rude, not yet at any rate, but he was tired and they weren't helping him. When Hunter's truck pulled into the drive, Lee stood up. Something had happened and Hunter was not happy about it. When he only stood by his truck, Lee went to him.

"You okay?" Hunter only stretched his neck muscles, and Lee grinned when he heard it pop a few times. "I'm taking that as a no."

"You remember that little fuck that works for Mrs. Schroeder?" There was that name again and Lee nodded, asking him if he meant the limo driver. "Yeah, that's him. I had to kill him today. I didn't want to, but he attacked a human for no apparent reason. I have a feeling that it's going to come back and bite me in the ass. I talked to Mabel too. She said that he'd been threatening her too. Fucking prick."

"No doubt." Lee tried to think of how to begin to tell Hunter of the conversation that he'd had yesterday with Lady Mantle. "I'm supposed to try and protect her. Not the dragon, but her grandniece. Lady Mantle, she came by yesterday and asked me to see to her. Help her out when she has issues. I don't know what's going on, do you?"

"No. Why you?" Lee could have taken offense, but he

only shrugged. "I didn't mean that the way it sounded. What I meant was, what does she think you can do for her that we as a pack can't do for her?"

"I'm not sure. I did ask her if this woman was my mate, and all she said was that she'd never met her. Did you?" Hunter told him what had happened today, and that the woman had been there when he'd arrived. "So he was hurting her. Great. It starts already. I don't suppose you know what she looks like, in the event that I see her in town and she's being hurt again."

"To be honest, I didn't see much of her. I knocked her back so she could be freed, because I was more concerned with the teeth snapping at my throat. I guess she might be pretty, but I'm sorry, I have no idea. Mabel saw her. She was having lunch at her counter out there at the airport when she called me. I guess she witnessed him being rude to this woman and called me in. And because he told Mabel that she was to stay out of things, I guess this woman stood up to him and slapped him in the face. I'm not sure she needs all that much help from a guy who makes quiche for a living."

"Ha, ha." Lee leaned against the truck as he looked out over the trees behind his brother's home. "I'm going to move into my house today and tomorrow. The stuff I ordered has been in storage, and I have some of the pack coming in to help me get it in the house. If you have time to come and help, I'm buying dinner."

"Steaks or pizza?" Lee told him steaks, and Hunter grinned. "I'll be there. Care if I bring Dad and the rest of them? I guess that Sloan is having a meeting of the minds with Addie, Jack, and Dawn over some of the things that had come up at her last board meeting. I guess Shawn is coming in too.

Clemmie is using him to look into some things."

"Great. The more I have to help, the quicker I can get moved in." Lee really was looking forward to being in his own home. Sloan had sent him some paperwork on the building that she'd purchased and asked him to look it over. He'd yet to crack open the file. "I'm so tired, Hunter. I mean, bone weary tired."

"You look it too. Even Dad noticed that you don't seem to be all here. What is it?" He told him he had no idea. "Maybe you just need to stop jet-setting for a while and simply be an Emerson. I'm sure that if you got bored Dan could find you some work. Ellis is busy, too, with his new pack. I bet either one of them could find you something to work on."

"Sloan too. She wants to open a higher scale restaurant here in town, and she wants me to run it. I'm not sure in what capacity, but she gave me the specs on it today." Hunter nodded and looked away. "What is it? You know something."

"No. Not really. I know that she's spoken to Shawn about finding a staff and cook to work it. You know how she is when she's got something in her head." Lee did know. "She wants this, and if you don't run it for her, I think she'll just find someone else to do it. Do you want to?"

"I'm not sure." Which was true. "When I got out of school, I wanted nothing more than to come back and make a name for myself in the best restaurant in Ohio. Hell, even the country. But I started doing this for Sloan and you, and all I could think about was that I was making a difference in someone's business. Not always a good impact, but a few of them we've been able to turn around. And all because of something that I did. Then when my blog thing took off and started being picked up by papers on what I thought of the restaurants that

I visited, I found that I really liked that. It's like my opinion mattered to some."

"You've always mattered to us, Lee. More than you know. And you like being in charge. That's the alpha in you." Lee shook his head. "Yes, it is. It's in all of us. Some more than others, but it's there. Look at Ellis. Not only is his pack doing better than it ever did, but he has a few members coming back to stay. That's what a good leader does. And I'm betting you're just like that too."

Lee had no idea but went to his truck an hour later intending to go home and rest again. But he swung by the diner to get some dinner and decided to see if Jarrett wanted to come over and eat with him. Luke ended up coming with him as well.

The three of them sat at one of the booths way in the back of the newly expanded place. The dinner crowd had yet to come in, so they pretty much had the back room all to themselves. Luke was telling them about his new son, Kelly.

"What a pistol. I'm telling you that Jack and I have to cover our mouths more often than not when he comes up with these amazing things he thinks he's saying right. He is adorable." His brother flushed before he continued. "I never thought I'd use that term in my life. Adorable to talk about a kid. But Christ, I tell you, I could not be more in love with the little guy. And he and Dad are going fishing tomorrow, and I'm so jealous that I can't be with them."

"You should bring him out to the house with you tomorrow after his trip. I'd really like to meet him." Luke asked him why he was coming to his home. "Oh, Hunter sort of kind of volunteered you guys to help me move some things out of storage. I'm hoping to move in tomorrow."

"That's great. We should make a day of it. I mean evening. I'll bring some desserts if I can snag some from Dawn. Ellis and she were in last week, and I have like five of her pies in my freezer. She said that she's trying out things and we get to be her guinea pigs. I told her to bring it on." Luke smiled as he continued. "I think, however, I need to cut back on having an entire pie by myself. My suits are getting a little snug lately."

When Mabel came back to ask them how dinner was, he noticed that she was looking a little tired too. He asked her if she was all right and she sat down with them. Lee had always loved this woman, and the fact that her and his dad were seeing each other was great.

"I was thinking about that new cart. I do love it. I could spend my entire life in it, just moving from place to place. Addie said she's having her company make me two more of them with different designs on them. I'm going to be her tester. I just love that woman." Nodding, Lee smiled at her. "But I hate having to interview people for working in here. Good heavens, you never know when they're telling you a fib or not. I'm having Addie come in tomorrow when I have these three come in for a job interview. She can tell me right off what's what. I'm going to have to hire someone to help out with the morning kids. There are so many of them now that word has gotten around. Even a few of those town kids."

He knew that Addie could touch people and know just what sort of person they were. So could her grandmother, but not as well as Addie could. She could do all sorts of freaky stuff when she needed to, and he was glad that she was willing to help out Mabel with her employees. For some reason his thoughts went to the woman that he'd been asked to watch over.

He'd done nothing to make contact with her. Lee really wasn't sure why he'd not done it when he'd made a promise, but as badly as he felt, he wasn't sure that he could handle anything else right now. Money wasn't a problem, though he wouldn't mind making more. And he had a nice home that he loved, but it needed more work. And then there was the.... Whining really wasn't something that he was proud of, but he knew that he'd been doing a lot of that lately and decided to stop.

When they all decided they had to get home, he went to his truck. He'd had groceries delivered yesterday, and had picked up the last of the few things he'd forgotten. Sitting in his truck, he tried to think if he could go one more day without milk and eggs, and decided he should get it over with and not have to get up tomorrow and go get them. He drove to the store and had gone inside with his cart when he saw the little girl.

He was just trying to decide if she was alone or if an adult was with her when she stood in front of the fresh tomatoes. He didn't care for them himself, but she was staring at them like she was going to be tested on their weight and color later. When she reached for the one closest to her, also the one on the bottom of a neatly stacked row, he grabbed it before she pulled it off the stand and toppled the entire display of tomatoes.

"Thank you, sir. I guess that was dumb. They should make it so short people can get to the really pretty ones, don't you think?" He only smiled at her and handed her two from the top. "I need three of them. She said that I had to replace the ones we ate. I only had one and a half, but the other one was bad so I threw it out."

As he handed her the third tomato, he noticed that she had the strangest items in her cart for a kid. There was a head of lettuce, a can of beets, and a banana. He asked her what she was up to.

"I have to replace what we ate on account of we don't have anything of our own. Momma said it's not nice, but she owns our hiney and we have to do what she tells us." Lee felt his wolf stir along his skin. The kid sounded like she was upset about what was said to her. But before he could speak to her about it, she continued. "Mom and me had a nice breakfast before she left me there, and that mean old bat came in and told me that we were freeloaders."

"Freeloaders. Why would she call you that?" The little girl moved to the front of the store, and he didn't want to lose her company just yet. "That's not a nice word, did you know that?"

"I didn't, but looked it up. I guess we are kind of. Mom is looking for a job that will pay us well enough to get out from under her thumb. I'm not sure what that means either, but I couldn't find anything about it in my dictionary." He briefly told her what it meant. "Oh. Well, then I hope she finds one soon, because she's about to crunch us to death with her rules."

Lee laughed, and the little girl smiled up at him. "You're cute. Where is your mom now? You shouldn't be here alone."

"I'm to do the shopping. I already told you that." He nodded but looked for her mom. "She's still trying to find someplace for us to live and a job. It's not easy for her though. I think people are afraid of her. I don't know why. She's the best mommy in the entire world. I think it's the old bat."

Before he could ask her why, he saw the woman up front

glaring at the two of them. Lee knew that it wasn't her mom, but she was eyeing the little girl like she was pissed to be with her. The little girl whispered to him that she was the cook where they were staying.

"She's making you buy this stuff?" She nodded, and Lee wanted to go to the woman and hit her for some reason. "She does know that you're just a kid, doesn't she?"

"I'm hoping so. I'm not very big, now am I?" He grinned again, despite his wolf wanting him to take her into his arms and protect her. "I got my stuff, mister, so I'd better get going. The old bat said I was to have my proper manners lesson today. Thanks for saving me a paddling."

"I'm sure your mom wouldn't have paddled you for knocking over a few tomatoes."

She only nodded at him and put her basket of items on the conveyer belt so that she could be rung out. As she was escorted out of the store by the cook, Lee watched her. She was carrying her purchases, and he could tell that it was sort of heavy for her. When they got to the car, he watched as she struggled with getting it open without any help from the woman to get in. Lee went to get his things. Standing in line, the cashier asked him if he knew the child.

"Not really. She is cute, isn't she?" Lily, a member of Hunter's pack, smiled at him and agreed. "I don't think she has a very happy life right now. Who would make a child shop for things that she's eaten? Do you know why?"

"No. The reason I was asking you is because she left her purse here." He looked at the small change purse that looked fat with change. "She gave me exact change, but she left it on the counter when she was picking up her bags, I guess. I thought if you knew her, you could give it back."

He debated with himself. If she came back to get it, he'd have it. If she didn't, then he wondered if she'd have to work off the money that she used and repay the person that was making a child shop for food. Lee told Lily that he'd make sure she got it. He had no idea how he'd do that, but he would. Taking the small change purse to his nose, he could smell strawberries and soap. Little girl smells.

CHAPTER 4

Kimber stood at the grill at four-thirty the next morning. It was hot now and she was waiting on her first order. Mabel, true to her word, had told her that she could work for her starting today and for as long as she needed. Kimber had never been so grateful in her life. And now that her daughter was registered for school, next week she'd be safe there as well.

Kimber tried not to think about her little girl having to use her own money to buy the things the two of them had eaten for breakfast. Or the fight that Kimber had had with her aunt after she'd found out. Her arm and back still hurt from the cane that her aunt had used on her when she'd dared to argue with her. Kimber brushed her fingers over the sore place and winced.

"And I suppose you think that I should simply let her eat me out of house and home while you're off doing who knows what?" Kimber told her aunt she'd been job hunting. "Of course you were. This had nothing to do with you not having to worry about someone to sit with the brat, did it? For all I know, you could have been laying with someone else to have another child that you think to bring into my home. Well, I won't have that either."

"I don't know anyone here well enough to sleep with them, even if I did want to. I think you've told enough people around here what sort of person you think I am. You do know that you've made it nearly impossible for me to get a job, don't you? Or is that your plan?" Kimber had been devastated when she'd been told at the laundromat where she'd gone to look for a job that her kind wasn't welcome. When she asked him what he meant, he called her a whore and slut. She'd left there, intending to go to the police about him, when she noticed that other people were moving to the other side of the street to avoid her. Not all, but enough to make her realize what was going on. "How do you expect me to make any money if you keep bad mouthing me?"

"Well, you could do it on your back if you wish. I'm sure that's how you managed to stay afloat all these years anyway. But you got caught once, didn't you?" Kimber felt as if she'd been slapped. "Get out of here. And know that I will keep a running total of all the things that you steal from me from now on too. Don't think I don't know that you had my driver killed when you got here. That alpha will pay for his part in your ploy to ruin me. I'll be tacking that onto your bill as well. The expense of having to replace him, as well as any incidentals that come from hiring someone to replace him."

Kimber looked at the woman standing next to her when she touched her arm. The smile was beautiful, but Kimber backed away from her. Her level of trust was pretty low right now. The woman—Kimber thought her name was Mary—handed her a slip.

"You were so gone that I wondered if you had on some headphones or something." Kimber took the order. "I'll get the toast for him. He likes it with extra butter. Cash is something else if you ever get to go meet him."

Kimber said nothing. She didn't want to meet anyone right now. A job and money had to be her first concern. But at the rate she was going, and the amount of rent her aunt was charging on top of everything else, she was going to be an indentured servant for the rest of her life. Hopefully, and this was her biggest hope, her daughter would be out long before Kimber broke down.

As she broke up the eggs for a western omelet, she wondered what her teachers at the college would think of her now. Kimber Gray, they'd told her, was going to be the best in the world. Now she only wanted to cook bacon crispy enough and the hash browns firm like requested for her very first short-order meal.

It took her less time to do the order than it did the toast to be done. Keeping it warm while she made two more orders, she tried her best not to think of anything but what she was doing. Four hours into her shift and at the end of the breakfast crowd, Mabel came to get her.

"Your little girl is here." Kimber tore off her apron, wondering what had happened. Mabel stopped her with a hand to her arm, right where the bruise was. When she cried out, Mabel started cursing as she pulled her sleeve up. "That damned woman. I swear to you…she did this, didn't she?"

"Yes. I have to go to Hannah, please?"

She went out to see her daughter, who had been put into

a booth near the counter. She was just sitting there, staring out the window, when Kimber said her name. Hannah launched herself at her, sobbing that she hated the old biddy. Kimber held her until she was quiet.

"She said that I was a bad person." Kimber lifted her little chin up to look at Hannah's tear-stained face. "I didn't do anything, Mommy. I swear to you. I was just sitting in the chair by the big fireplace and listening to my book. She tore it from me and threw it in the fire. Why does she hate me? Then she told me to get out of her room. It wasn't her room. I asked the cook. She hates me too. But I wasn't doing anything. I even had on my headphones like you told me to when I was there. She's just mean. I think she has that stick up her bottom like you told that one lady."

When Hannah started crying again, Kimber knew that she wasn't going back. There was nothing at that place that she couldn't replace, and her aunt would just have to sue her if she wanted her money back right now. Kimber was glad now that she'd never signed the papers that had been put in front of her last night when she'd gotten home. But for now, she had to care for her little girl.

"Do you think you can stay here while I work, baby? I need to finish up my job so I can keep it. Then you and I will go and find us someplace else to live. I know that your bunny is there and you love him, but I don't want to go back there and I don't want you to either." Hannah told her she would be all right without it. "I'm so sorry, Hannah. I didn't mean for you to be hurt by her."

"I don't want to go back, ever. I know you said we can't go home, but can we maybe try?" Kimber told her that there just wasn't any money for it. As she sat there holding her, Mabel came and sat across from her.

"I can't go back there." Mabel nodded. "And I don't have anywhere to go. I just don't know what to do."

Mabel patted her on the hand and got up. Kimber knew that she was going to fire her, and she really didn't blame her. She was sitting on her ass with her sobbing child in her arms when she should have been working. When Mabel returned, she had a stack of coloring books and three boxes of crayons, as well as a box of what looked like crafting items. Kimber felt her eyes fill with tears as the elderly woman talked to Hannah.

"You have yourself a nice little work place here, child. And when Mom is done for the day, we'll see about getting you two a safe home. Do you think you can do that for me?" Hannah nodded at her and sat on the seat. "Did you have something to eat? I can have Mom here whip you up something. I've been having nothing but raves about her taters. And Cash was beside himself with his omelet today."

"I didn't have any more money for food, so the old bat wouldn't let me have even a piece of toast today." Kimber looked at Mabel when she drew in a sharp breath. Kimber explained to her what had happened yesterday. Hannah spoke when she'd told her what had happened, all of it. "And I lost my purse too. Fern gave that to me for my spending money, and I can't find it. I wonder if she took that too. The old bitch."

"Hannah." Kimber was trying her best not to laugh, but she'd hit the nail on the head with the description of her aunt. "We don't call people names like that. And that's a bad word."

"Yeah, honey, even though it fits her, you shouldn't call people that." Mabel winked at her. "I have a few nice names I'd like to call her myself. When I'm alone."

Hannah said she'd be fine, and Kimber went back to

work. Every few minutes she'd go and check on her, and was nervous that every time she did, someone was sitting with her. She asked Mabel about it when she came in for a plate of food.

"Oh, they're keeping an eye on her. There won't be nobody going near her that I don't approve of. I've taken that little thing under my wing, and nobody is going to hurt either of you again." Kimber could only nod. It was nice to be told that, but she knew her aunt. She'd get what she wanted at all costs. And Kimber was actually afraid of her.

At about eleven-thirty, Kimber took Hannah a sandwich and some chips. She was chatting away to an elderly man, but he only winked at her. Mabel was sitting with the two of them or Kimber might have asked him to move on. He appeared charming, but they were always the kind of people you had to look out for. After that the orders starting coming in, and she never looked up other than to see what was written on the paper in front of her.

"Hello there." She turned swiftly and looked toward the male voice that was behind her. Kimber didn't speak, but she did nod at him. Christ, he was huge. "I'm Hunter. We sort of met yesterday."

"You look different today." He laughed, and she was still trying to figure out the joke when a lovely woman came into the kitchen with him. She looked ready to explode, she was so heavy with her child.

"I'm Sloan Emerson. Mabel told us you needed a place to stay that was safe." Kimber nodded again. "You're not very talkative, are you? But that little girl of yours is. She's just the cutest thing. I understand that you're the niece of Kimberly Schroeder. Is that right?"

"Grandniece. And please don't hold that against me. I

don't think I could take much more in bad vibes today. I—my daughter and I have only just moved here from France." Sloan nodded and smiled as she rubbed her belly. "When are you due?"

"Three weeks and counting. We're having a girl too." Kimber congratulated them both. "Thank you. But about your living situation. It just so happens that we have a nice little cottage here in town that is empty."

"I couldn't. I'm sorry. But Hannah and I are going to have to think of something else. I don't want to be rude, but we're a little on the...we're in a tight way, if you want to know the truth, and I don't think we're going to be any richer in the next few hours. But I do thank you." She didn't want to think of the shelter that she'd called, but that was all she could afford right now. "I really appreciate you thinking of us, but money is low right now."

"Be that as it may, you still need a safe place, even if it's just for Hannah. And you don't know what the rent will be, so how do you know you can't afford it?" Kimber started to argue but was cut off when Sloan spoke again. "Don't lie to me, Kimber. If you don't have something, or have something to say, then say it. I find it annoying when people beat around the bush."

Kimber let her temper soar. She rarely did that, having a tight control over it and her mouth, but she'd had a really shitty week so far and a crappy life too. When the woman smiled at her as if she knew what was going on, Kimber let it go.

"All right, I'm broke. The fact that I get a free meal here with each shift I work means I can feed my daughter today with the little money that I had with me when we got here.

We had to sell everything that we owned. Next week, or even tomorrow, I have no idea, there might not even be any of that left. The school where she's been registered wants me to pay her dues. I'm not sure what sort of dues they think she might need with only three weeks of school left, but I can't get her tested for her grade level until I pay the twenty-four dollar fee for that as well." Kimber wiped at the useless tears. "I was fired from my job because I did a better job of doing it than the man that was too drunk to do it on his own. And when that happened, because money is forever tight when you're only fourth chef, I could no longer live in the house that we had since my daughter was born, and had to beg my bitch of an aunt to help us out. Now, not only do I have to pay her back for the tickets for us to come here, but she's making my child, my eight-year-old little girl, pay for her meals while I'm not there. According to my aunt, I'm going to have to pay for every meal we eat, in addition to the rent. And let's not forget about the money I'm paying back to her for a man who attacked me the other day and was killed for it."

Kimber turned back to the grill. She was hurting all over. Not just from the beating she'd taken last night, but she was broken inside as well. When arms wrapped around her, to no doubt toss her out the door, Kimber screamed at the pain. The man standing in front of her wasn't one she knew, so Kimber backed away from him.

"Don't." She stilled when Hunter spoke to her. "This is my brother, Lee. If you run, he's going to shift. And this is not the place to let that happen. We're going to be calm and rational, aren't we, Lee?"

"I just want to go." Hunter was looking at Lee, so Kimber looked at Sloan when Hunter ignored her. "I'm all right now.

I just…when you touched me, you touched an old wound."

"When did they happen? I'm guessing that they're less than twenty-four hours old and that someone beat you with her cane." Kimber nodded at her, not sure how she knew. "I know, Kimberly. And that cane of hers is famous. But I would ask that you put your hand on Lee's arm. It would go a long way to calming his wolf."

"I don't know why you'd think I could do anything to calm him. I'm barely calm myself." Sloan moved closer to her and Lee growled deep in his throat at her. "What is wrong with…what the hell is wrong with you?"

Grabbing the man by the arm, she jerked him around to face her. There was fury there, and she nearly backed away from him again. But she could see his wolf and knew that Hunter had been right…he was close to shifting.

"He hurt you." His words were slurred, and she wondered if he was drunk on top of everything else. "No one will touch you."

"Really? And how the hell do you expect to make sure that happens? In the event that you need to be told, I'm a grown woman and can take care of myself. Not very good, mind you, but I have been trying." He growled at her this time. "Oh, do grow up. He didn't do anything to me. I came here like this. And while I do appreciate you thinking you have to be all macho and stuff, I don't need you or anyone else leaping in where you shouldn't. She's too…my aunt takes no prisoners."

"Schroeder?" Kimber nodded. "You're her niece? The woman I'm supposed to protect?" He looked at his brother, who only shrugged at him. When Lee turned back to her, she could see that he was now pissed at her.

"I don't know what you're talking about. Why would you

think you have to protect me? And from whom? My aunt?" He nodded, then shook his head. "That wasn't helpful at all. I don't know who you are or why you think I need your protection, but I'd rather you just stayed out of my life. I have enough crap going on, and you won't be helping yourself by getting yourself wrapped up with me."

"I'm your mate." Kimber heard his brother start laughing behind him, and then the door opening and closing, shutting them off from the dining area. "I'm sure you know what that means. I'm going to make sure that you're not mistreated any longer, and see that you have a place to stay. I was talking to Mabel, and she said that—"

"She had no right to tell anyone what was going on with us." He asked her who the *us* was. "My daughter and I. We're having a rough time right now, but you're not needed. Like I said, I have enough going on for several lifetimes, and I don't need some bossy dick coming into my life to make it worse. So get the hell away from me so I can do my job."

Turning her back on him, she had a moment to worry when he growled again, but his mouth was suddenly at her neck and he was nibbling on her throat. Her body seemed to have been thrown on a live wire as soon as he moaned in her ear.

~~~

Lee felt his wolf stir along his skin. He wanted his mate right now. And his wolf also knew, as he did, that she'd been hurt. Running his hand gently down her waist to her hips, he pulled her back against his body as he explored her neck. Christ, she was hot and delicious.

He'd come into the kitchen to see if Hunter needed him. It wasn't like Hunter—or Sloan, for that matter—to go into the kitchen, and he thought that if they needed him, he was there. But he'd seen the girl doubled over in pain and Hunter reaching out to touch her. His wolf must have smelled her before him, because he was ready to kill Hunter before he knew what was happening. Then he was standing close enough to get her scent.

"I don't think you're supposed to be back here." He pulled her hips closer and rocked into her firm ass. "Please don't do this. I can't afford to lose this job too. You have no idea how much I need it."

"I need you more." He moaned when she whimpered. "I'd like to sit you on the counter and strip your pants off and feast on you. Then take you somewhere that I can make love to you all night." He worked the tiny buttons free of their confinement on the front of her blouse, and then cupped her breast before working to free her more.

"I can't let you do that." Lee cupped her naked breast in his hand and rubbed his thumb over her hard peak. "Please don't do this. You can't want to have sex with me right now."

"I'd love to have sex with you right now. And later, then again after that." He nipped at her skin hard enough to draw blood, and sucked on the tiny wound. *You taste like sex to me. Let me take you out back and see if all of you tastes like that.*

Lee felt her respond. He could smell it on her too. She was wet and needy. But before he could reach into her pants and touch her, someone cleared their throat behind him. Lee turned just enough so that they couldn't see her and how he'd nearly undressed her. He'd managed to get her blouse undone and her bra lifted up over her breasts. And if he'd had his way, her panties would be on the floor as well.

"Kimber, honey, I have some people wanting to work. Do

you need a minute or two?" Lee told Mabel yes, but Kimber told her no. When the door closed again with Mabel's laughter going out the door with her, he kissed Kimber on the neck again.

She jerked her shirt closed, and he stepped back. He wanted to show her how easily he could get her naked again, but he doubted that she'd be any happier with him. With her hands holding her blouse closed, she turned to him.

"Get out of here." Lee thought about telling her that she was coming with him, but saw the look in her eyes. "I don't want you to come near me again. This is…do you have any idea what my life is right now? How much shit that is—?"

"I met your daughter yesterday." Her face paled, and he took a step toward her but stopped when she glared at him. "She was buying food at the market. I'm not sure of her name, but she left behind her purse. I have it. Your scent is the same as hers. Strawberries. She's cute, by the way. And looks like you."

"She had to replace what she'd eaten." Lee nodded. "I didn't know she'd made her do that. And when I found out, she…she told me that she's going to keep track of what we eat. I don't want you to think that I make my child do slave labor. And she won't again if I can help it."

"You can't go back there." Kimber nodded. "I have a big house. It's not…I'd very much like it if you stayed with me."

"I'm not going to sleep with you. And I'm certainly not going to live with you. You think that just because you…you nearly had me naked, that I'm easy? Well, I am not." He nearly laughed at the tone in her voice. He supposed he could have been offended, but he really just thought it was cute. "You…I don't even know why I let you…let you do this to me."

"I'm not sure either, but I enjoyed it." Her face turned red. "But as for my house. I would very much like for you to sleep with me, but I know that we have to get to know each other first. It's a big house, lots of rooms. You and Hannah could even share a room if it would make you feel better."

"You make it sound as if it's a foregone conclusion that we'll end up in bed, or that we'll just do as you say. Well, I won't. I might be desperate right now, but I won't trade one hell for another. Thanks, but I don't think so." One of the dishwashers came in the room with them then, and snorted as he passed them. Lee only watched him, knowing that Hunter had more than likely told him what was going on. "I don't have any money to pay rent either, but Sloan said she had a cottage."

"You'll both be safer with me. I can promise you that. I know your aunt, and if she finds you, what do you think she's going to do to you? I don't want you to pay me...you can help out around the house if you want. You don't have to, but you can if it makes you feel better. And the yard. I'm having flowers delivered in the next few days. You and Hannah can help me by planting them." She looked at the grill and the two orders that had just been hung there. "I can watch Hannah for you while you work too. I won't harm her any more than I would you."

"You say that I'm your mate. How do I know you're not just saying that? And so you know, I have known a few mates in my time, and one of them didn't end well. The people across from us were supposed to be mates. She murdered him, then killed herself." He moved toward her with his hands up. Lee asked her to put her nose against his throat. "And what will this prove?"

"If you're my true mate, you'll understand once you smell me. And so you know, the couple that you were talking about? They weren't mates. You cannot harm me any more than I can you. They might have been lovers, but not mates. Not true mates." She didn't look convinced. "I swear to you, I won't touch you while you test my theory."

Lee didn't think she was going to do it. As another order was placed on the ring in front of the grill, she put down the spatula that was in her hand and took a step toward him. Even before she did as he'd asked, he could tell that she was closer to believing him. And as soon as her face was at his throat, her mouth at his pounding pulse, Lee felt his entire being center, his heart calm, and his wolf rejoice at finding her. Perhaps this was what he'd needed all along. But when she stepped back from him, he could see she might need a bit more convincing than he or his wolf did. She was still not going to trust him.

Lee

CHAPTER 5

Kimber walked around the house. It was beautiful. A little empty right now, but she told herself that the furniture was coming soon. She had no idea why, but she thought that she'd like his choices in that as well.

The kitchen was made for someone who enjoyed cooking. The island in the middle was huge, and the sink at the one end wasn't the kind that was just for washing hands, but big enough to wash the pots and pans that hung over it. She glanced up at the double hanging pot rack and felt her fingers itch to touch them. But she only walked to the double refrigerator with a matching freezer next to it.

"I have a large family and they like to eat." Kimber nodded to Lee. He picked up Hannah and sat her on the counter. "I wanted to show you my stash. I love these kind of cookies. And if you want, you can have as many as you want. If Dawn comes over and has a basket, we, my dear child, are going to be in heaven."

"I'm not allowed to have too many sweets." But she took three of them from the box when he offered. "Can I really have as many as I want? I'll pay you for them if you get some of those coconut kinds."

"Macaroons." Kimber looked at Lee when he said it at the same time she did. "She can have one now and the rest after dinner. You know how I feel about ruining your dinner, Hannah."

Kimber thought that he'd tell her she was too strict on her daughter, but he only took the two extra she had in her hand and put them on a small plate. Lifting her off the counter, he hugged Hannah before putting her on the floor again. Hannah held his hand while he showed them around the rest of the kitchen.

"I hate to carry laundry up and down the stairs, so I have a washer and dryer here and one on the second floor. They're both large capacity because I wasn't sure how the smaller ones worked with a family." He opened the pantry for her, and she moved into it with him. "This has another freezer in here, as well as a storage center. I'm not really sure I'll ever use it, but Dawn, my sister-in-law, told me that I needed it. So I put it in."

As they made their way out of the large area, she felt his mouth brush over her neck again. He'd been doing that, touching her in some small way, since he'd picked her up at the diner. While it wasn't anything that she was used to, she hated that she was enjoying it so much.

They made their way to the dining room. "This table came with the house. I was so excited about having such a large one that I didn't think about how much room it took up in here.

So we knocked out the outside wall here and expanded the room by ten feet. The windows were Jack's idea. She said it was friendlier than just having walls that said nothing about where the house was. And if you want curtains up, we can do that, but I love the view that we can have while we eat."

"You listen to your sisters-in-law a lot. They're right, but you depend on them a great deal, don't you?" He nodded and walked to the large built in corner cabinet. There was nothing in it, but he told her that they would hold a lot of dishes and linen when it arrived. "I'm guessing that you'll entertain a lot when you get settled."

"Yes. When we get settled I hope we can entertain a lot. If you don't want to, that's fine too." He kissed her neck again and moved away as he spoke. "I know that it's only early May, but Sloan wants us to have the Fourth of July picnic here. She thinks we should be ready by then. What do you think?"

Kimber didn't answer him. She had no idea where she was going to be in two months. For all she knew she might be in prison, or worse. Kimber also wanted to tell him that she'd not moved in yet, and that making plans like it was a done deal was just dumb. But she really did love his house.

The next room that they went into was the family room. She supposed it might have doubled as a ballroom if need be. It was the biggest room she'd ever been in. The hardwood floors were gorgeous, as was the wainscoting on the walls. It wasn't the fake kind, but real oak and walnut.

A fireplace took up half of one of the walls. It was sitting right in the middle of large glass floor to ceiling doors that were open now, with the early spring breeze blowing into the room. This room, like the others, had no furniture at all, but she could see that it would easily fit several couches, as well as a few wingback chairs. A large television, still in the box, sat in one corner of the room, and she could see that the size of the room would easily accommodate one that size. To her, it looked as big as a king-sized bed. Maybe the bed would be smaller.

"We like our football. And I thought if we wanted to watch some adult films together, we should go life size." He laughed when she looked at him. "I'm kidding, Kimber. My brother Hunter bought the television for me...for us. He said it was a housewarming gift. I think it's his way of saying I was going to be holding the game day here. It's because I usually make some mean snack food to go with it. Do you like football?"

"I do. But I enjoy the food, like Hunter does, more. It's fun to find things that go well with company." She thought of her other job. "When I was working, there were times when I got to make the side dish for the night's meal. It was the most fun I had working there, next to the appetizers. I have some amazing ideas if you want to use them." He told her he would like to, very much so.

The office and study were next. He told Hannah that she could come in here, but if there were papers on the desk, she wasn't to touch them without someone telling her she could. Hannah looked at Kimber as she spoke to Lee.

"My mommy says that too. She has all these recipes that she's making up and works on them at home, with Fern and me as her testers. Sometimes she makes them just for me to try. I get to rave them." He told her rate. "No, rave them. I don't have to eat like those people do in the restaurant. I can just taste what I want and rave about them."

They all laughed, and Kimber was caught off guard at how easily it had come to her. When Lee wrapped his arm around her waist, she knew he was being careful of her back when he didn't jerk her around. It was hurting her badly now, her back was, and she was tired too.

As they started up the stairs, several trucks pulled into the driveway. Lee went to the door and told her that his family was here already. When she went to look at them, Kimber had a moment of panic. There must have been seventy people there.

"They're pack too. Hunter said he was going to bring a few with him. But if he's expecting us to feed all these guys steaks, then he's nuts." Another few trucks pulled in and women started to pour from those as well. "Okay, maybe we don't have to feed them all. The women have arrived to help out. This is going to go fast."

"Hi." Kimber nodded at the woman who was carrying a large bowl of what looked like potato salad. "I'm Jack. I don't cook, but I was told to take this to the kitchen. Can you point me in the right direction?"

Kimber nodded and they made their way back to the area. Even as she entered the large room, she noticed that someone had come in the back door by way of the yard, and there were enough people in the kitchen to run a well-oiled restaurant. As they began pulling on aprons, Jack asked her where the playroom was.

"I don't...I have no idea where he's going to put one. Or if he will." Jack only nodded and told her for now they'd used the study. Kimber took her there. In no time there were playpens set up, toys all over the floor, and a dozen or so young girls organizing the ten or so kids that seemed to pop out of nowhere, her daughter among them.

"She'll be just fine. This is mine and Luke's son, Kelly.

He's six, just a little younger than Hannah." The little boy shook her hand, then darted off to play with the kids. Kimber looked at Jack. "You're very overwhelmed right now, aren't you?"

"Yes." Jack smiled and asked her if she could give her some advice before the others got there. "There are more of you?"

"Yes. We're mates to Lee's other brothers. There's Addie, who you should not touch unless you want her to know everything there is to know about you, including things you might not want her to know. Don't tell Sloan your ideas unless you want her to make them a reality. And Dawn…well, don't piss her off. She doesn't have a temper or anything, but you might not get some of her jelly when she makes it. And that would just suck."

"And you? What should I avoid about you?"

Jack seemed to consider it, and then smiled at her. Kimber thought that this woman would be the scariest of all the women she'd just been warned about.

"Me? I'm as sweet as they come. Really, you have nothing to worry about." Yes, Kimber thought, she was scarier than anyone.

~~~

"Where is she? My grandniece, where is she right now?" Kimberly's butler only stared straight ahead, not even making eye contact when he told her he did not know. That was the way she liked things, normally, but she was mad and he'd better have some answers for her. "And that brat? Did you drop her off at the diner as I instructed?"

"Yes, my lady." She asked him if she cried and threw a fit. "No, my lady. She told me to have a lovely day and went inside on her own."

"Well, I'm not having a lovely day." Kimberly slammed her cane down on the floor for effect. "Where is she? I do not like not knowing everything, Daniel. You are to find her or… never mind. I'll do it myself. Bring the car around."

As she made her way to the front of the house to go to the police station, she had Daniel bring her the file on her desk. This was getting out of hand. First, Kimber just up and moved to another country. Then she joined that college that Kimberly had forbidden her mother to let her go to. And then, in what Kimberly could only think of as pure stupidity, Kimber had herself a child that she could not afford.

When Daniel told her things were ready, she looked at him. "No matter what I do to bring her down, she manages to land on her feet. First, I have her wages cut at that restaurant I had to buy. Then I had that man across from her try to break in. And what does he do? He tells her he's sorry and brings her things back. What am I paying these people for if not to do as I have said? Then the crowning glory was that man who gave her the brat. When the heck is this going to go my way?" Daniel said nothing as he helped her on with her coat. "She'll heed me now or I will ruin her and that child. Perhaps that's where I need to look. That brat will need to go."

The ride to the police station wasn't long, but she hated to travel. There was a time when all she needed to do was make a simple call and things would be just as she wanted them. That Conklin man, he would nearly foam at the mouth to do her bidding. And the sheriff as well. Both of them were gone now, and she'd been blindsided by their being arrested.

As soon as her car stopped in front of the station, she told the driver to wait for her where he was.

"You mean to wait right here?" She looked at the five cars she was blocking that were parked legally in their spaces. One was a cruiser, but the rest were cars that had no business taking up her space when she came to town. "I guess I can move when they need out."

"You'll do no such thing. I want you right here. And if you as much as move forward an inch, I will fire you and have your license revoked for failure to listen to me. I make the rules here, and the sooner you figure that out, the better you'll be able to keep your job." Kimberly was smiling when she entered the building. Having things her way was the only way, and everyone knew it. And if they didn't, then they would soon enough.

"I want to see the sheriff." The man at the counter looked confused, so she snapped at him. "Now, young man. I'm too busy to wait until you have your brain work through this. Sheriff. Now."

He finally picked up the phone and turned his back on her. She wanted to pop him on the head with her cane. The glass between them would have made it difficult, but she could have worked around that. But she noticed that everyone was staring at her, and Kimberly only liked that when she wanted it. Today, she did not.

"He said to tell you to have a seat and he'll come out and get you." Kimberly told him to tell him to come out now, and the kid actually told her to have a seat. "He said to have you wait for a minute until he's done with his business."

"He's in the bathroom then." He shook his head no and pointed to the chairs to her left. "No. I shall wait right here."

There were others behind her now. Two men that looked like they'd just robbed a bank and had not gotten away. And a woman that she could smell all the way to her point in the line. She was high on something. Kimberly thought about her grandniece, and thought that would be a good way to rid herself of the brat. Kimber would be made to be a drug user.

The man behind her poked her in the shoulder. "Hey lady. Why don't you have a seat before you fall over?" She thought it was a threat and turned to use her cane on his head. "You don't even want to do what is going through your head right now. You might make others piss their pants when you speak, but I'm not like everyone else."

Fear, an unfamiliar emotion, ran down her spine. He didn't really look that large, but he was threatening. Instead of hitting him, as was her intent, she turned back to the man behind the glass wall and glared at him. He, however, was ignoring her in favor of the book in front of him. Before she could point out that her taxes were paying him to work, not lollygag, her name was spoken. The man, the new sheriff that she had not approved of, opened the door for her to follow.

"Miss Schroeder, what brings you down here on a lovely day like today?"

She paused before going into his office. The grin on his face made her think he knew something. Bringing her cane down on his foot hard made him wince, but he said nothing. Nor did she.

"I want you to arrest my grandniece. She's robbed me and I would like her brought in to face the consequences of her actions. I have the paperwork right here." As the sheriff sat down, she noticed the man sitting on a smallish couch in the corner. "I do not need for others to hear my grievances, sir. I want him out of here now. I don't know who hired you, but the sooner you figure out that I get what I want, the sooner we'll get along just fine."

"No. He's with me and he stays." The sheriff didn't even bother looking up at her when he spoke. "He's here on other business, and since you're here with contracts, he might be more useful than you can imagine. By the way, I'm Max Rogers and this is Luke Emerson."

She was perturbed when the sheriff handed the file to the other man. Emerson? The name sounded familiar, but she had no idea why at the moment. The longer he studied the file, the more upset she became. Kimberly was used to people just doing as she said.

Kimberly felt out of her element. There were no servants around to do her bidding. No one was bending over backward to do what she said. And the man behind the desk seemed more interested in the computer in front of him than he did having her in his office. Of all the nerve. She picked up her cane again, and that was when the Emerson man finally spoke. From the look on his face, she had an idea that he knew just what she was thinking to do with it.

"What is it that you're claiming Miss Gray stole from you? All you've given me is a contract between the two of you, and neither of you have signed it." She huffed. "Is this a copy and you have the signed copy elsewhere?"

"First of all, I did not give you anything. He did. And no, that is not a copy. She has refused to sign it. I have put it out on her dresser three times for her to sign, but she said that she would like a lawyer to read it over. There is no reason for her to waste more of my money on such a thing. I have it the way I want it, and she should just simply do as I say." The man laughed. "You're not to laugh at me, young man. I will have you fired from your job as well."

"You had her fired from her job?" Kimberly tried to think how he'd gotten that information, but he started talking again. "You never said what she stole from you. And this contract? It's a little one-sided, don't you think? I mean, you are charging her fifty percent interest on this loan, as well as a monthly fee of two thousand dollars for room. Anything that she eats, you're charging her for. If she brings in her own food, you're charging her for storage. Laundry fees, even if she does her own, are being issued. If I were her, I'd have someone look this over too. And I would advise her not to sign it. Smart girl, your grandniece. I like her."

"Well, it's a good thing that you're not her lawyer, isn't it?" He tossed the file on the desk and smiled at her. Kimberly turned to the sheriff again. "He is not to speak to me again. Or I will go over your head to have this taken care of. I might yet. You have no idea of the power I can have with a simple phone call."

"I'm sure you think you do. And as for you going over my head, he's sitting right there. This is our mayor. If you wanna go over his head, then I'm thinking you'll have to go to Sloan Emerson, his sister-in-law. She has more power than you will ever have...if you mean money, that is." Kimberly knew the name Sloan. And she hated that woman as much as she did her grandniece. "I can see by the sour look on your face that you know Mrs. Emerson. Good, that will save us a great deal of time in this pissing contest that you've started."

Kimberly didn't care for the way he was speaking to her. And less so the way that the other man, this Emerson person, was smiling at her like he knew more than she did. No one did. She prided herself on knowing everything on everyone.

"I want my grandniece arrested for taking my money."

He asked her how much and when she noticed it was missing. "The amount is right there in the contract. She took it when I sent it to her."

Both men looked at each other before Emerson spoke again. "You're claiming that she took the money that you sent her to come home on? You do know that's not stealing at all, not when you have given—"

"I have given her nothing. I have tried and tried to bring her to heel, and now that she's here where I want her, she's brought that brat with her. I will not tolerate having my rules broken. And she will heed my wishes or I will do more than just have her pay cut and her home robbed." Kimberly knew the moment that she closed her mouth that she'd gone too far. "What I meant to say is, she has had her pay cut and her home vandalized."

"No, I'm pretty sure you said it right the first time." Emerson stood up and stretched. Kimberly wanted to back away from him, but the chair she was in blocked her from doing that. But she did want to get as far from the man as she could when he leaned into her, only inches from her face. "You're to leave Kimber alone from now on. And if you as much as come near her little girl, I will harm you in ways that will make the beating you gave Kimber look tame."

"I don't...you have...what are you talking about?" He stood up and so did the sheriff. "You will not speak to me that way. I am Lady Kimberly Leta Schroeder, and I will have your respect."

"I don't care if you're the fucking president of the United States. You harm my family again and there will be hell to pay." He paused before leaving the office. "And the 'Lady' part? Yeah, you made that up. You're no more a lady of any kind than I am. I have my ways of looking into everything and everyone too. And stay the hell away from my family." The door didn't slam, but it sounded loud in the quiet of the room.

Kimberly tried to think what he'd meant. Not just the lady part. He'd been right about that. She'd gone to England one summer and had come back with that title. Not given to her, but she'd given it to herself. What did that matter to him anyway? But the family part was something she didn't understand. As much as she hated to do it, she demanded that the sheriff tell her what he'd meant.

"Since you asked so nicely and all, I'll tell you. Kimber is going to marry his brother. She's living with him now, so I don't think it will be long before he weds her."

Kimberly sat there. When she found her tongue, she glared at him.

"She will not be marrying anyone that I don't say that she can. She's mine." He laughed. Not just a small one, but a laugh that rang through the room and bounced back at her. "She is my ward. And she will listen to me, or I will make her life not worth living."

"Is that a threat toward her?" Her entire body froze up. His humor was gone now and he looked...he looked murderous. "Because if it is, I'm going to come after you and make sure that you know the meaning of a pissed off wolf if you do anything to anyone from now on."

A wolf. This man was a wolf. As she rose up, leaving the office, all she could think about was he was a wolf. A wolf that did not like her, nor did he feel the least bit intimidated by her money and name.

Kimberly was in her living room, not having a clue as to how she'd gotten there, when she realized something.

Not only was the sheriff a wolf, but she was pretty sure that Emerson was as well. Even that bitch Sloan.

"Oh, I've stepped in it now," she said to the empty room, and wondered what to do to have things the way she'd wanted from the moment she figured out that Kimber's mother had gone against her wishes with her will. She had to get her grandniece here. That was important for the rest of her plan to go through. Things were too far along now to try and do anything else. Not that she would, but there was a well laid out plan, and they were going to follow it or else. Also...as much as she hated to do it, she'd have to contact Sloan Emerson. That woman would be able to convince this other rabble what she wanted was right. And if not right, perhaps she could convince her that Kimber marrying into her family was a bad idea. Kimberly would make their life, if they deemed to have one, worse than the one that Kimber had had in France all this time.

Control. It all came down to controlling someone. She'd had to work as best she could while Kimber had been in that other country, but that had been a complete failure. The school had been first. Then there was the man that Kimberly had made sure Kimber dated. He had paid dearly for his mistake, and the child, his child, should never have been. But now that she was here, home, Kimber would do as she was told or there would be hell to pay. Just as the Emerson man had said. First things first, she'd have to call Sloan and demand her help. Whatever happened after that was...well, things were going to go her way or she'd know the reason why.

CHAPTER 6

Lee loved the way everything was turning out. He kept an eye on Kimber, but he knew that she was in good hands. And Hannah was having a good time too, he'd noticed every time he'd gone into his office to put a box in there. Kelly was helping her with the names of all the other children.

"Mr. Lee?" He looked up when Hannah said his name. "I have something I need to ask you. It's really important. But I don't want Mommy to know."

"Okay. But just so you know, your mom will have to know if it's something that will get us into trouble." Hannah crawled up into his lap and he looked at Hunter, who was taking a break with him on the back deck. His brother just laughed and asked Hannah if he could be there too.

"Yes. I need to talk to you too. But Mr. Lee is first." Lee nodded and told her to just call him Lee. "Oh, no. I can't do that yet. You and Mommy aren't a person."

79

"Person?" She nodded and explained what she meant. "Oh, an item. But we are. You are a part of our item too. I'd like for the two of you to live here."

"Yeah, that's what I wanted to talk to you about. Kelly told me that he has his own room with his stuff. I don't have anything. Not here. There's no bed for me, and I don't have any clean clothes. I know how to wash, but I don't have anything to wear while I do them up. Will I have to go to the…Mommy said I can't call her bitch, but I won't have to go there at nights, will I? She's not nice, and I can't have my reader when she's around."

"Why not? I mean, why won't she let you have your reader when you're there? As for your things, we'll figure something out. And I've ordered you a bed. I hope you don't mind, but I got one that you can grow into. Your room is pretty big." He wasn't going to touch her calling her aunt a bitch. For one reason, he agreed with her description, and second, he wasn't sure how to correct her if her mom already had.

"She said that it's not fitting that I have something like that when I owe her so much money. I tried to tell her that it wasn't costing her anything and I was just reading it, and she took it from me. She just threw it in the fireplace and melted it all up. Why would she do that to my things and she don't have to replace them, but I have to replace my food?" Lee looked at Hunter, who sat up. "Mommy bought that for me with the last of our furniture money so I could be special."

"You are special, darling." Hunter looked in the yard as he spoke in a low but tense voice. Lee could tell he was trying his best not to upset Hannah, but she was already there so he tousled her hair for her. "See that man over there? The older one making everyone listen to his dumb jokes? Go on over there and call him Grandda. I'm sure if you do, and tell him about your reader, you'll have one before tomorrow."

"Really? But that's cheating and not nice, isn't it? I think Mommy said that it's…manipulation. I think." Hunter told her that he was going to be her grandda as soon as her mommy and Lee were an item. "Really? I'll have a grandda? The same one that Kelly has?"

After she left them, Lee tried to wrap his mind around harming a child like this woman had. And even though she'd not done so physically, she had hurt her. When Hunter stood up and started to pace, Lee watched him. Hunter was scary upset about this too.

"She needs to break ties with this woman. Now." Lee said he knew that too. "Luke is on his way here. He said that he had a run in with her, this Schroeder woman. She went to the station and wanted to press charges against Kimber for the money she loaned her to come back here."

"I'll pay it." Hunter nodded and then shook his head. "You're not paying it, Hunter. I know that you think that you should for some reason, but Kimber and Hannah are my responsibility."

"I agree, but that's not what I meant. I don't think you should pay shit until we figure out what's going on. I have a feeling that there is more here than we think. Maybe even more than Kimber knows." Lee nodded and stood up. Break time was over. But Hunter stopped him before he moved off the deck. "I'm going to have some extra patrols for a while. I don't think she'll come here, but you never know. And when Kimber goes to work, have Mabel watch out for her. I'm worried that…something isn't right about this."

When Sloan came out of the house with her phone to

her ear, she smiled at Lee. But it was tight and he knew that something had happened. When she sat down and pointed to his chair, he and Hunter both sat. He smiled when she winked at him.

"Oh no, Mrs. Schroeder. I think I understand what you're saying to me. You think you have to have her under control. Why is that?" The phone was laid on the table and put on speaker. There wasn't anyone around them, but he knew that Schroeder would be able to hear if anyone came up on the deck. "Now, what was it you were telling me again? I guess being as far gone as I am with this baby, I've missed a few things."

"Baby? Oh, you poor thing. Why on earth women let men do that sort of thing to them is…well, I'm very sorry that you're in that way. If you need someone to help you rid yourself of it, just let me know. Lord knows I have a lot of friends that find themselves in some situation or another that need my help." Schroeder laughed and it sounded manic and forced. "I was saying that I demand that Kimber come back here. I've heard some rumors that have her staying with one of your husband's family members. That just won't do. She's my ward, and I have taken it upon myself to make sure that she's well cared for."

"I'm pretty sure that Lee will care for her very well, but I thought that when someone was your ward it was only until a person reached a certain age. I'm not sure, but I think that Kimber is well beyond that by now." There was silence at the other end. "Besides, Kimber has her own child to care for and she's doing a good job of that. Such a wonderful little—"

"That issue should never have been born." Lee started to reach for the phone, but Sloan smacked his hand. "I told him only to pretend to fall in love with her. Darn it. Does everyone have to do things just the opposite of what I pay them to do? I simply told him to make sure that he had her in his life, then to bring her home. But he called me months later, just when I was ready to have her back here, and told me he was going to marry her, of all things. That was not what I wanted. Do you see what I'm up against? Now not only do I have to take care to bring Kimber to heel, but I have to contend with that brat as well. He was very careful not to tell me about that…that thing until it was too late for me to do anything about it."

Lee heard a slight noise and turned to see Kimber standing just on the steps to the deck, and Hannah was with her. Before he could move to hold her, she put up her hand and he stopped. Sloan started speaking as he watched Kimber.

"I have no idea what sort of plans you had in mind, but I want you to know right now that you're on my shit list. You were before, but now you're right at the top. And that is not a place to be. About the brat, as you have called her? She is very precious and wonderful. As is her mother. So you know, if you want to take me on about them, then by all means, try me." Sloan stood up, her belly nearly taking her back to the chair again, but she held onto the table and leaned into the phone. "Kimberly Schroeder, you have just fucked yourself royally over this. And I'm going to make you rue the day that you tried to hurt one of mine." The phone was not just closed, it was tossed into the yard. Lee thought if she could have, Sloan would have leapt over the deck railing and torn it up as well.

When Lee pulled them both into his arms, lifting Hannah up to his shoulder, he knew that Kimber was close to losing it. Hannah started crying first, her tears burning into his skin as badly as her pain tore at his heart.

"I had no idea...."

Lee held Kimber when she started to cry too. Taking them both into the house, he had no idea where to go. There were more people in his house right now than he had seen in months. Moving to the pantry, he closed the door behind him and turned on the light. Kimber clung to him as she sobbed hard.

A few minutes later, there was a brief knock at the door. He told them to go away, but his dad said that he'd like to talk to Hannah. Lee didn't want to let her go, but Dad said he had to talk to her. When Hannah left them, climbing into his dad's arms much like he had when he was a child and hurt, the door was closed again.

"She hates us. Hates...how could she do that to us? Why? I never did a thing to her other than...just to come here. I hated to call her. I had no idea that she knew James. And he worked for her?" Lee let her babble and held her. "When I had Hannah, all alone because he had been...Lee? Do you think she had anything to do with his death? I wouldn't put anything past her now. She is evil."

"I don't know, love. But she went to the station today and Luke was there. I guess she was going to press charges against you for stealing from her." Kimber said she'd never taken a thing from her. "The money that she lent you to come here on. She said you stole it. Luke is coming here and he'll explain things better."

Kimber pulled away from him and started to pace the tiny room. "She said our rent would be two grand a month. And there would be a fifty dollar a week fee for my laundry. Not that she was going to have it done, but she was going to charge me for it anyway. And our food. I could eat with the kitchen staff, but that would cost me seventy-five dollars per meal. But if I wanted to have my own food that I would cook for Hannah and I, that would cost me more. Storage fees were ninety dollars a day, use of kitchen was fifty per meal, and then there was the cost of our part of the electric and water. I would never have been able to save to move out on our own. I think that she had planned it that way. To keep me...she wanted me to never leave, yet she hates me."

"I don't know, Kimber, but we'll figure this out. I promise." Kimber nodded, and Lee felt his wolf run along his skin. He was pissed off and wanted to hunt the older woman down. "I don't want to piss you off more, but when you got here, Hunter had some things investigated. Not just you, but your work too."

"I'm sure that was enlightening to him." He nodded. "What did he find out? I'm sure that it wasn't all that good now that I know a few things about my aunt."

"Not all, no. Your checks where you worked, you were only getting half of what you were to be paid. The other half went to your aunt here in the States. Also, your rent was doubled where you lived, as was most other things that you had bills for."

Kimber sat down on the floor and he went to her. Picking her up, he sat her on his lap while she sat quietly. He was worried about her now. He knew that perhaps he should have told her in a better way, but he liked it straight up and didn't think to soften the blow.

Hunter told him Luke was here. Lee told him he needed a few minutes, and Hunter told him to take his time.

"She made it difficult for us. There were months when it was pay the electric or the rent. I had to go without food for days sometimes so that Hannah could eat. I tried so hard, Lee. I wanted a better life for us than…my mother was a good woman, but she was so terrified of my aunt." He held her while she cried again, and was wondering if he could have the pack go and murder the fucking bitch when Kimber started talking again. "When Mom told me that I could go to Europe to study, it was a dream come true. After a few weeks there, my aunt called and told me to come home. Demanded that I do as I was told and to get back home. My mother called a short time later and said not to, begged me not to. Not ever. And I had no intentions of ever coming back. Even when Mom died, I nearly did, but then I got a call from Mom's attorney. He said that my mother's wishes were for me to stay away. Forever, if I could. It was the hardest thing I've ever done."

"She was trying to save you." At Kimber's nod he pulled her face to look at his. "I'm sorry, love. I truly am. And so you know, neither you nor Hannah will ever be hurt by her again. I promise you this with all my heart."

"I don't know what to do."

Several ideas came to mind, but he didn't voice them. Marrying him was one. Another was to let him take care of this. But he knew that she had to do this on her own. Not to mention, if he tried to do this for her, his sisters-in-law would kick his ass. Smiling, he turned her head to see him.

"What do you think about going out there and running all the family and friends off? Then I take you upstairs and ravish you until you can't move. Then for good measure, I do it again, just in case I missed something." She laughed a little. "Are you a screamer? We might have to put our room just a little further away from Hannah's if you are. I don't want her to think I'm hurting you when you come down my throat."

"Does this always work for you? Seducing women with your charm?" He told her he hadn't ever tried it before. "You expect me to believe that you've never tried to charm a woman into bed with you?"

"No. I've never had to seduce a woman into bed with me." Kimber smacked him hard on the shoulder. "Well, I haven't. Is it working with you? Because I have to tell you, I'm hard as a rock and need to be inside of you in the worst kind of way."

To prove his point, he pulled her around so that she was facing him and rocked up into her. Kimber put her hands on his chest. He was sure it was to stop him, but he cupped her ass and brought her closer to him until she was riding him.

~~~

Kimber wanted to stand up, but she also wanted to continue what she was doing. When he put both his hands on her ass and pulled her to him tighter, she moaned at the sensations of having his cock so close to her pussy.

"I can smell you. You're wet and aroused. Take off your blouse for me. Let me suckle at your nipples while you ride me." Lee groaned when she cupped her breast over her blouse. "Feed me, Kimber. Let me taste you while you take what you need from me."

"I'm so close now. This is so wrong, but I need this. And I feel like you're the only one that can satisfy me." He told her he would be from now until forever. Taking her blouse up and over her head, Kimber held him to her breast as she fumbled with the back clasp. He was driving her crazy. And when he lifted her bra up and out of his way, the feel of his mouth over her skin made her wrap her legs around his hips to get better leverage.

"I want to take you right here." He rolled her to her back,

and his cock was grinding against her now. Kimber wanted to come with him, feel him inside of her when she did. Reaching between them, she moaned when she felt his cock instead of the snap of his pants. He so was full and hard, he filled her hand and she knew she needed more. "If you touch me right now, I'm going to take you, and damn the people who can hear us."

"Please." He tore her pants off. Her body wasn't on fire as much as it felt scorched by him. Everywhere he touched her, each brush of his fingers, brought her skin to life. And when he sat up, pulling away from her, she reached for him only to still in her movements. "You're beautiful."

His cock was in his fist, his juices streaming from the tip in a long thick cream. The crown of his cock was dark, his shaft long and hard. Running her finger over the tip of him, catching the precum that was there, she took it to her mouth and licked it off, and only looked at him when he moaned.

"You should see you the way I do right now." Lying back, she cupped her breasts in her hands, tugged at her nipples, and her body grew wetter knowing that he was watching her. When he took just the tip of her breast into his mouth, she lifted her hips up to take his cock into her. The crown of it just sliding into her heat had her coming hard and quick.

When he took her, slamming forward hard enough to take her breath away, Kimber bit into her hand to keep from screaming. Wrapping her legs around him, her feet locked behind his back, she held him to her, digging her nails into his flesh as his cock pounded her. When his mouth moved down her throat to her shoulder, Kimber tilted her head, giving him whatever he wanted, knowing that she was taking more than just his body. And when he bit her, tore into her throat,

Kimber screamed out, her body bowing up off the floor as he commanded her to bite him as well. Sinking her teeth into whatever she could reach, Kimber tasted his blood, felt his cum fill her even as she felt her vision blur and blackness reach up and slap her out.

Opening her eyes, she knew that she'd not been out for long. He was still atop her and his breathing was still harsh and hot against her neck. When he lifted his head, looking down at her from a short distance, Kimber kissed him gently on the mouth, then pulled him back to her.

Lee rolled to his back and she went with him. His cock was still inside of her, and she could also feel that he was still hard. Sitting up, she watched his face as he held her hips still when she tried to ride him.

"I'm going to take you again if you keep this up." She told him she hoped so. "You're going to be very sore later. I'm not able to hold back when you scream my name like you did."

"Fuck me. Or let me fuck you." Her movements were quicker, her body burning to feel him fill her again. "I want to come this way. I've never…this isn't something that I've done before."

He held her to him, his hands, strong and firm, digging into her muscles. Kimber wanted him to take her again, roll her over and fuck her like he had, but the thought of coming like this, feeling the power she had over him right now… Kimber didn't think there was anything more erotic. Leaning down to his nipples, she nipped at first one then the other as Lee lifted his hips into her. When she found herself on her back again, he lifted his body from hers again and she reached for him.

"Not yet. My wolf, he wants you." She started to shake

her head when he was suddenly gone and his wolf was there. Kimber started to back away from him when he buried his head between her thighs and licked her clit.

Nothing could have prepared her for the feeling of his rough tongue on her pussy. He ate her, licking her to three orgasms before she finally reached down and curled her fingers into his fur. It was soft, silky, and warm.

Come for him again. He loves your taste. She came again, her body so worn out she could do no more than cry out. When his mouth changed, the fur in her hand suddenly gone, she looked at Lee as he took over where his wolf had been. Kimber begged him to stop. Pleaded with him to please let her rest, when his fingers slid into her pussy again and he touched off something that made her scream out his name once more. Then everything was gone.

This time when she woke, she was in a bed. There weren't any sheets on it, but the thick comforter was wrapped around her tightly. Struggling to get at least her arms out, she realized that she wasn't sore like she'd thought she'd be, and that she, incredibly, wanted Lee again.

The envelope with her name on it that was leaning against the lamp had her reaching for it.

"Love, you have no idea how much I'd like to be waking next to you right now instead of finishing up the move. But if we get this done, then I can join you. I wanted to tell you that Hannah and my dad are together. He's taking her to dinner and then they are going shopping. I can't even begin to tell you how much that frightens me. My dad is not known for his shopping abilities. But he will protect her with his life.

"There are some clothes for you in the bathroom. Sloan brought something for you from her house to wear since I tore yours to pieces. Damn, woman, you are amazingly wonderful.

"Come down when you're ready. I think that dinner is at six, but if you miss it, the ladies said that they'd make sure that all the leftovers are put up for you to enjoy later."

Looking at the clock, she saw that it was just after five. Feeling stupid that she'd been in bed for nearly three hours, Kimber got up to take a shower. That was when she realized that she was living here.

The shampoo and soap, while not manly, were his. The large sponge was obviously new, but she could see that it was too big for her small hands. There was no razor in the stall with her, but there were two toothbrushes. One of them was still in the package and the other very used. Taking the one with the wrapper still on it, she made a mental note to get herself a new one to replace his. Getting out, she reached for the warm towel just as someone knocked on her door.

"It's Dawn. We met today downstairs." Kimber told her that she was dressing and would be out in a second. "Do you mind if I talk to you like this? I wanted to get you up to speed on a few things."

"Sure." Dawn told her good and then was quiet. As Kimber pulled on her bra and panties, a new set that she'd never seen before, she asked Dawn if she was still there.

"Yes. I'm trying to think how you want this. Straight up? Sort of around the bush, or are you the type that likes details as you go along?"

"Straight up, with a little around the bush if you please." Dawn laughed. "You're making me very nervous. Is my daughter all right?"

"Oh yes. She and Dad got back a little bit ago. And so you know, we just love her to pieces. You did a wonderful job with her. She's adorably polite, and she just says it like it is." Kimber opened the door, holding onto her socks that had been with the rest of the clothing. "It did fit. Good. I've never been very good at it, but Sloan, now there is a shopper. I'm sorry. I should just get to it."

"Yes. But thank you about Hannah. She's my joy and I love her with all my heart." Dawn sat down when she did. "You were going to tell me something."

"I was. It's about...I'm to tell you a little about us. The Emerson women. Sloan wanted to do this, but she had to take a nap. The baby is wearing her out. And Jack said that she warned you a little, but she can be scary sometimes, don't you think?" Kimber nodded. "Anyway. Sloan first. Do you know who she is?"

"I do. Even in France, where I've been the last few years, I read about her interview with the newspaper. I don't know how she did it. But she's the one that was hurt by her stepmother when she was a child. And she's rich."

"Right. It's really Addie that I'm here about. She wanted me to tell you if you don't want her to intrude in your mind that you shouldn't touch her." Kimber paused in pulling on her socks. "She can read your mind, your future as well as your past. She wanted you to know that. I think...I'm pretty sure that she doesn't have to touch you to read you, but she's at least polite in asking you if you want what she can do."

"And if I don't want her to know, then what?" Dawn looked away. "She already knows, doesn't she?"

"Yeah. Your aunt is one crazy fucking bitch. And she's going to kill you."

CHAPTER 7

Cash tried to figure out what his newest grandchild was telling him, but he was too distracted by the conversation that was going on across the room. Kimber was trying her best to hold her tongue, quite well as a matter of fact, but she was getting more and more upset with them all just the same. When she looked at him, he nodded to her and stood up, putting Hannah on the chair where they'd been sitting. It broke his heart to leave the child, but he'd get more of her loving later. She was just the sweetest little thing he'd seen in a while.

"You're not helping her." They all turned and looked at him when he stood in front of her. "Look at what you're doing to her. She's about to explode like a bag of manure did last summer when it laid out in the hot sun too long."

"I'm not sure I like being compared to a bag of manure, but you're right. I'm overwhelmed right now." He sat down on the heavy table that he'd help put together not an hour ago when Kimber started talking again. "There's just too much."

"'Course there is. Now, this here is what we're going to do." He looked at Lee. "He's gonna hold onto your hand and then Hunter is going to talk. When it's too much, what he's telling you, then we'll move onto something pleasant. Like…I don't rightly know, but you can think up something."

"I want to talk to Addie." He nodded, then frowned. "I know that she can…I don't want to die."

"Not going to happen. You tell her, Addie. Things in your visions, they can change, can't they?" He hoped he was right, and when Addie nodded, he could have kissed her. Might even later, after Jarrett was gone again. That boy was a might possessive. More than the rest of them were.

"So I might still die, but maybe not." He nodded at her. "That's not helpful at all. I think…I have no idea what to think right now. I have a family that I never bargained for…not that I mind having you all here, but there are so many of you. When Hannah and I were living in our apartment, it was just her and me and Fern, my housemate. Now it seems I have five brothers-in-law, four sisters-in-law, a nephew, and a niece on the way. You, Mr. Cash, as well as an entire pack that will protect me with their life. And you want to know what the funniest part is? I'm not even married."

Her laughter was a little on the manic side, and Cash could understand that. He took her hand in his and said her name until she looked at him. Fear was there, and the overwhelmed feelings she'd been talking about. But Cash could see her inner strength too, and was glad for it.

"You wanna marry my Lee?" She didn't answer him. "I can see where you'd be a little upset on that front, but you two have already mated and bonded. You know that, don't you?

So marrying like humans do ain't really that necessary. But we do it for the things that the law says we need to have. Like insurance, for one thing, and property. Understand?"

"Yes. Dawn explained it to me. She also said that you all would be able to smell it on me." She glared at Lee, who grinned like a fool back at her. "Someone should have explained that part before the pantry."

"The pantry?" Cash felt his face heat up when she got red in the face too. "You'll have to forgive me, child. I'm just so proud of my boys for finding the right mates. And making sure that they're marked."

"I don't want anyone to get hurt on my account." Cash wanted to tell her that wasn't going to matter if she needed them, but she lowered her voice as she continued. "I don't just have me to watch out for, I have my daughter too."

Cash looked over at the child. Good heavens, he'd fallen in love with her the moment she'd come up to him and asked if he really was her grandda. And taking her shopping had been the most fun he'd had in ages. He was looking forward to more outings with Kelly and her together. He had a feeling it would be a hoot. Cash looked back at Kimber.

"You don't have to worry none about her either. That girl has my heart almost as if she'd wrapped her little hand around it and took it from me. And that Kelly? Those two are going to get in the best kind of mischief, and I'm going to be right there egging them on." Hunter laughed, and he looked at him. "You tell her, son. Tell her that we're never going to let them get hurt again."

But Luke cleared his throat, and Cash nodded. She did need to know what she was up against so they could start keeping them safe. When he started to pull his hands free of hers, she held him tightly and he stayed right where he was. Cash had a feeling that of all his daughters-in-law, this one would take some convincing that she was stronger than she thought she was. Making sure that Lee was all right with him holding her hand, his son winked at him and he could have burst, he was so proud at that moment.

"Your aunt has some things lined up for you that you need to be made aware of." Mrs. Mantle, Addie's grandmother Clemmie, came into the room then, and Luke waited until she was settled before he continued. "The things that you overheard today, that was only the tip of the iceberg on what she's done to manipulate your life. Some of it…most of it isn't even legal."

"She killed James, didn't she? Or she had someone do it." Luke nodded, and the fingers on Cash's hand became painful for just a second. "He tried to tell me that he'd been doing things that he wasn't proud of. But I was so happy with him and the baby that was coming. He kept Hannah's conception from her on purpose, I guess."

Kimber kissed Hannah on the head when she came to sit by her mom, then asked Cash if he'd mind taking her into the other room.

"Sure enough. Me and this one, we got us a mean game of some candy game going on. And I'm not even disappointed to find out that there's no treasure at the end of it, am I, sweet thing?"

"You're silly, Grandda."

His heart did a little flutter every time she said that to him. Kelly had started calling him that too, after Hannah had told him that was her name for him. Up until then he'd been calling him Cash. Grandchildren were the way of the world as far as he was concerned.

Cash wanted to be there for Kimber, almost needed to be there, but this was important, shielding this little one from the terrors that her aunt was bestowing on her. When they were settled around the conference table in Lee's office, she looked at him and he was almost afraid.

"My mommy is hurting in her heart, huh?" He told her that she was at that. "I wish I could fix it for her. I don't like it when she's hurting. She's the best mommy in the whole wide world."

"I think you might be right there, darlin'." She toyed with the game piece a little more, and he decided to just talk to her for a bit. "You know that my son, Lee, won't hurt you two, don't you? He's about half in love with your momma now, and he's about to bust, he loves you so much."

"He needs to be all the way in love with her. She needs him to love her more than anything, even chocolate. My mom... she thinks I'm the only one that will ever love her, and I think that's just sad." Cash nodded. "And he has to marry her too."

"I agree." She played with the little plastic piece that came with the game. He watched her, wondering if she'd tell him the rest, but she only sat there. "What is it, honey?"

"I want to be a wolf like Lee is. Kelly said he was one already. I want to be a wolf like they are." Cash had no idea what to say about that, so didn't say anything. "Can you fix that for me? Kelly said that he'd do it when I was older and all. On account of me being his mate. I don't know what that is, but he said he would protect me forever. But I thought I'd be better at it now."

"What?" She nodded and picked up the die to play. "When did he tell you this, darlin'? You're too young to be anyone's mate."

"I'm his to protect and he'd take care of me. I told him I was able to save myself. But if I needed somebody, there wasn't going to be nobody else but him." She tossed the die out, and he watched her count out the number of moves. "I'm going to love him until forever. It's your move, Grandda."

Cash couldn't help it. He laughed so hard that he hurt from it. Picking up the little die, he tossed it like she had and then picked up the card that went with it. He was still laughing when he had to move all the way back to the start.

~~~

Luke handed the file, much thicker than the one that Kimberly had given him this morning, to Kimber. The only difference was, everything in his was true. And it wasn't nearly as prettied up either, just straight up information. He watched Kimber, and while she looked at the newspaper clippings that he'd printed, he started telling her what he'd found, being mindful of Sloan, who slept on the other couch.

"When your mother died just after you left for France, there was a lot of speculation that she'd killed herself. There are still a few that believe that, but she didn't. I have a couple of contacts in the county, and her death certificate is still pending. I have no idea why it's not filed with just unknown on it as cause of death, but it's still in her file. And that is why we think your aunt wants you here."

"My mom was sick. I mean…she had cancer, but it was just the beginning stages of it. The doctor said she'd be all right for a while if she had treatments. Could that be what killed her?" He shook his head and sat down. "Then why do *you* think she was killed?"

"First, I need to explain something to you. Your mom

was the sole heir to the estate of your grandda. Did you know that?" When she shook her head, Luke knew that he was on the right track. "He had inherited his money from his dad, and him from his. There was a great deal of money there when your great-grandda died. Millions of it. But your grandfather made more, doubled it and then some. When he died, the will was read in a private office with just your mom and the attorney. She got it all. Your aunt, his sister, got nothing. And you were named as the heir to your mom's estate, while your aunt got nothing. But she is able to live in the house that she's in until such time as she dies or you decide to take it over. She can neither sell it, renovate it, nor can she do anything other than maintenance to it unless you allow it and approve it in writing only. Which, I'm sorry to say, you have been. Or so the attorneys for the estate thought."

"I don't understand. I've never had to give my permission on.... My mom didn't have any money. She had to borrow money from the bank to send me to school." Luke shook his head. "Yes, my aunt told me when I came home that she'd had to pay that outstanding bill, and I had to pay her back for that too. She showed me the paperwork."

"There was no loan because she didn't need to borrow anything. I've gone to the bank and had Hap look into it for you. He said that he'd have it in the morning. But I can tell you right now that the money that your mom took was from her own personal account." Luke handed her the current balance sheet from the bank and the account her mother had. "The reason your aunt needs you home and under her thumb is because without you, she cannot get to the money in the bank. Among other things. The insurance policy that's in your name isn't doing her any good, because she needs someone to sign off on the death certificate. Once that is done, she'll do the same to you as she did to your mother...have you ruled incompetent. I think that's why she hates you having a child. Instead of her inheriting everything, as she would because you are all she has left, Hannah would get it all."

"You think she killed Mom and made it look like she'd killed herself, don't you?" Luke nodded. "Why would she do that to her? Why not just keep my mom around when she had all the money? And why did my mom not tell me about it?"

"I don't know why she did it, but I know how we can find out." He looked at Addie when she did. "Addie would only have to touch her and she'd know everything. And while I'm not really keen on using her powers for most things, I think, as do the rest of us, that you deserve to know. If your mom killed herself, then I will tell the old bat I'm sorry. But I don't believe she is as innocent as she wants us all to believe. Not that she's made any sort of bones about being a real bitch about everything, but on this I think she has plans that will ruin you, and harm Hannah too."

"She's not innocent at anything. And I think we all know that." Luke smiled at Kimber. "When I got here, she gave me these contracts. There were...one was the rent that I'd have to be paying to her, and there was another one. One that...let me get it. I kept that one."

When she left the room, Addie moved to sit near her grandmother. The two of them had their heads bent together and Luke looked at Hunter. Nothing good could come of the two of them conspiring, and he was pretty sure that Hunter thought the same thing. When Kimber came back, she not only had the contract, but she had a thick file of her own.

"This is all the conversations I've ever had with my aunt.

Dates and times too." He looked at the file and the copious notes that she'd written. "I don't know if you can use any of this or not, but there is also a sort of signed confession from James. We were never married, so you know, but I did have his name put on the birth certificate. He was...I don't think we were in love as much as we were very happy. Does that make sense to you?"

"Yes it does. Who's to say you wouldn't have fallen in love had there been time? But I'm glad you had each other. As for you not marrying him, I was getting to that too. You should know that as of this morning, James Walden's parents have been notified of his daughter's existence. I didn't do it...I believe your aunt did. And I don't think they're going to be happy with her when they find out that everything they were told about you and Hannah is untrue." Kimber asked if she'd painted her to be a horrible mother. "You have no idea."

"I've been searching." They all turned to Addie when she spoke up. "It's something that I do when I feel an injustice has been done to someone I've come to admire. And you should know that not only did your mother not kill herself, but she was leaving to come to you when she was killed. Your aunt didn't kill her, but she paid someone to do it. I just think...you should know what she's capable of."

"My mom was coming to me? To France?" Addie nodded at Kimber. "How did she...she had called me the week before she'd died. I...it's all in there. She told me that she couldn't take her aunt any longer and that she needed to cut the ties now before it was too late. I just thought she meant before she died. I never...how did my mom die?"

"Suffocation. Your aunt pulled some of her strings and had it down as natural death because of her cancer. There was one man, one that wouldn't be bought off, that thought her accounting of your mom's death to be wrong. He filed a report with the state. He was dead a week later. The report is still in the system. Finding it should be no problem for Jarrett."

"She killed him too." Luke didn't say anything. He thought that Kimber's statement was correct also. "What do I have to do to end this with her? I mean, we don't have anything like hard evidence on her, but we can…I don't know. I want her to be out of our lives once and for all."

"I'm glad you said that." Hunter moved forward on the couch and smiled at Kimber. "We're going to take the old bitch down. And I think that doing it by using you is the best plan."

"Oh no, you're not. You'd pitch a bitch if we suggested using Sloan for something like this. I'm not allowing you to use Kimber." Luke closed his eyes when Kimber stood up. Lee did as well while he continued to dig the hole he'd opened deeper and deeper. "You know how dangerous she is. What's to say that she won't try to kill you too? Or take Hannah? I think the best thing we can do is send the two of you to Dawn and Ellis's home and hide you there until we take care of this."

"Why? Do you think I'm incapable of taking care of me or my daughter?" Luke watched his brother, telling him through their link to just shut up and tell her he'd been wrong. "You think that because I've had such a shitty life because of her up until now, that I should just roll over and let someone else fix this?"

"That's not what I meant. I just meant that you're not as equipped to do this. We're wolves and we're stronger than—"

Luke winced when Lee's head snapped back from the blow, knocking him back to the couch. Kimber had delivered her punch to his face like a real pro, and he was proud of her.

When Lee started to stand, Hunter put his hand on his leg. Lee didn't move.

"I'm sorry." It was too little too late, Luke thought, and when Kimber stormed out of the room, no one moved. Lee looked lost, and Luke almost felt sorry for him. Almost. "I think I fucked up, didn't I?"

"I think you're underestimating your level of fuckery on this one, but hey, I tried to tell you."

Lee looked like he'd lost everything. And if he didn't fix this, it was going to be a long night for him. Luke told him to get up and get into town.

"For what?" Then he stood up. "A ring. I need...I need two of them. I have to...will you stay here until I get back? Of course you will. Thanks."

He was out the door before anyone said anything. Hunter started laughing first. Then Luke did. He wondered aloud how far Lee was going to get before he realized he didn't have any shoes on. Then the door slammed again and they heard him running up the stairs. Hunter laughed again.

"He is so fucked right now."

Even Clemmie laughed that time, and soon they all were. When Lee left the house the second time, Sloan woke up. When they told her what was going on, it was all Luke could do not to go and find Jack and tell her too.

"I've been wondering something. I think perhaps you can help me." Luke nodded. If he was honest with himself, he'd tell her that he was too afraid not to help Clemmie. Her laugh made him embarrassed. "You do know that I'd never hurt what I consider family. The Emerson men and women mean a great deal to me. All of you."

"Thank you." She nodded. "I'll do what I can. I know that

we've found someone to help you out with a few things, and I believe that you're enjoying it here in my little burg."

"I am. And that's what I wanted to talk to you about. I know that Sloan has a bee in her bonnet about opening a new restaurant. I like that idea, bringing culture here to your little burg, as you called it. But I want to bring in some art. Not the kind at the Louvre, but local and some state things. I know of a couple of struggling artists that would love it."

"I can see about property we can...you have a place in mind?" Her nod was sort of funny, as if she were up to something. "I'm almost afraid to ask."

"I'll have to wait and let you know. I do know that the person who lives in it now will be vacating it soon. And it will be such a lovely open place to have arts displayed." He had an idea she was talking about Kimberly's home. Clemmie grinned. "You are a very smart boy. But let's not say anything to Kimber. She has enough on her plate for the moment."

When she stood up, telling him that she was going to see if there were any of Dawn's lovely scones left, he turned back to Hunter. Then when something occurred to him, he turned back and said her name.

"Will Graham be happy or pissy about this new artist that you have coming to town? The reason I ask is because I don't think Graham has it in his head that he wants or needs a mate. He's pretty set in his ways." She only smiled at him and left the room. Luke turned to Hunter again. "I think we might be all mated before the end of this year."

"I hope so." Sloan had fallen asleep again, and Hunter put his hand on her swollen belly. "I can't tell you how happy I am. And you know what a fool I was about this whole mate business."

"You were insane." Hunter nodded. "There are other things we need to talk about when you have time. Not really pack related, but it might come to that."

"Is it the warehouse renovations?" Luke told him it was. "I've been hearing that the renovations are going well, but they're having some issues with squatters and the homeless. Don't they realize that we're doing this for them? If they don't help out by moving to someplace until we're finished, we can't finish."

"Where will they go?" Hunter said he was working on that too. "I think, and you can say no if you want, but I think that the building a street over would make a great temporary home for them. We have the cots and the blankets. Sloan got a great deal on those when this project started. But until we can do something for them, we're going to be fighting this forever. Some of those people, Allen was telling me, have been there for years. It's all they know."

"I can have a crew come in today if you want." They both looked at Sloan when she spoke. "And a temporary kitchen. Mabel said that we could use her old things that she had moved out when she renovated last month. Maybe that will go a long way into having them move."

Luke grinned at them both. "And you know what? I think I know the perfect person to run it for us. Mabel said that Kimber is the best grill person she's ever hired. This would go a long way in helping her transit to the restaurant you're opening. Because you know as well as I do, she's been the one you had in mind from the very beginning."

"I don't know what you're talking about." When Sloan stood up, she turned to Hunter as she continued. "Can you get this going for me? I'm hungry enough to eat a bear or two."

As she left them there, Hunter laughed. "She's always hungry. And I'm glad. At least when she has this baby, she'll have enough strength to do it. Christ, I cannot wait until our daughter is here."

Hunter left him then, and Luke started for the office to see if he had missed anything at the office. But instead, he heard his son laughing with his dad and Hannah, and went to find out what sort of things they were getting into. He wondered, like he had so much in the last few days, why he'd not found his mate sooner. Being in love and being loved was the greatest thing in the world.

CHAPTER 8

Kimberly watched her attorney, Tate Walker. The man was driving her insane the way he kept making notes, then humming. Like that was supposed to give her some clue as to what he was going to do about this ridiculous lawsuit filed against her. The nerve of some people. When he finally leaned back in his seat and looked at her, she wanted to bash his head in with her cane.

"I'm not going to ask you if any of this is true." Well, there was that, she thought. "However, if even one thing on this list of grievances is correct, you'll be facing jail time."

"No, I won't. Because you're going to fix this. And if you don't have the balls to do it, I will." He sat up and leaned his arms on his desk. "Whatever it takes. You just tell me who filed this against me, and I'll make sure that they change their minds."

"Kimber Gray Emerson." Kimberly felt her temper, never

a good thing on the best of days, flare up to where she felt it all over her body. "And her attorney is not one I'd mess with. Shawn Connor is the best there is. And not only that, he has more money to back up his claims than you do. He works for Sloan Emerson."

"Kimber is not married to him. Or that other man either. I made sure of that one." He picked through the file that he'd had when she arrived and handed it to her. It was a marriage certificate stating that Kimber had married Lee Emerson, dated yesterday. When he handed her a second sheaf of papers, she only tossed them back at him "She did not have my permission to marry anyone. I want this nullified now. What am I paying you for if you're just going to inform me of these indiscretions and not do a thing about them?"

"You know that I can't do that. She's over twenty-one and no longer considered your ward. Though how you managed to have that paperwork signed off on is not something I want to know about either. She's an adult and has been for some time. And if someone were to look at the paperwork that made her your ward back then, you'd be in trouble for that as well. You'll have to do what they want or face more prison time." Kimberly lifted her cane. "You should also know that we're being recorded. And if you hit me with that again, I will be adding my name to this list. Being your attorney has been bad enough; I won't be abused by you again. In fact, here you go."

She took the paper. Reading it over quickly, she nearly tossed it back in his face. But Kimberly smiled at him before she spoke. No one left her employment unless she said they could.

"You owe me a great deal of money. And I know that you're unable to pay me back, so this is useless." He handed her a check. It was made out to her, and for the amount that she knew he had borrowed from her to finish college all those years ago. "What is the meaning of this? I know that you do not have this kind of money. And if you think to give me a bad check, I'll tack on more charges. Stop this right now. You are not leaving me until I say so or you're dead. Would you like to know which is going to come first?"

"That's a personal threat, and I won't stand for it. But the money? It's not a personal check but a certified one. And I have the money because I borrowed it from someone." She asked him who and he leaned back in the chair and smiled. "I'll not accept this. You still work for me until I say differently. Now tell me what you're going to do about this…this lawsuit that my grandniece is being forced to use."

"I'm no longer your attorney as of the moment you took that check." The door opened behind her and she turned to see his secretary standing there. "Mrs. Engel, could you please make sure that Miss Schroeder makes it out of the building safely? Not just her, but anyone she might encounter as well. She does have it in her nature to harm those that cross her path when she's…upset."

"You'll pay for this, Tate. I won't be treated this way. You'll regret this." He asked her if she was threatening him again, and she picked up her cane and slammed it over the desk. "You're darn right I am."

Kimberly had it in her head to hurt the girl that was showing her out. But the man standing there with his hand on his gun made her think he'd shoot her without a single bit of hesitation. Kimberly was sick to death of all of these fools, and they were going to pay for treating her this way.

When her name was shouted, like she was nothing more

than a taxi driver being hailed, she turned to tell off whoever had dared call her by her first name. But she saw Tate coming toward her, and she knew a wonderful kind of pleasure. She was going to make him grovel before she allowed him to come back to her.

"You saw the error of your ways, have you? Well, don't think that I'm going to just forget your small lapse in intelligence." He shoved a file at her and she had no choice but to take it. "What is this? I don't have time for your foolishness, Tate. Just say that you're sorry and I'll try to forgive you."

"But I'm not sorry. In fact, I'm excited as hell that I'm free of you." He nodded to the file in her hand. "That's your file. When you find a new attorney, if you can find one after today, he's going to need that. It also includes the paperwork filed against you that you asked me to look into. And again, you're on camera, with witnesses that you received it."

He turned and walked away from her. Kimberly wasn't sure what was going on, but the whole world seemed to be plotting against her. Making her way to the door, she tried to wrap her mind around Kimber doing this to her. She seemed to have inherited some of her mother's backbone that she'd finally shown at the end. Well, she'd take care of that soon enough too.

As soon as she came out of the building, she looked around. Cars had been parked in front of the building when she'd gone in, and the limo that she'd had parked behind them was nowhere to be seen. If he drove around the block and made her wait for him, she'd have him fired and everything else she could think to have done to him for making her stand here like some sort of street walker.

"Where is my car?" She turned to the guard who still had

his hand on his gun. "I told him to park right here and not to move. What have you done with it? I'm not a happy person right now, so I would tread lightly with me." He laughed and she wanted to hit him as well.

"It's been impounded. You can't just block the street like that. There are laws that you have to follow like everyone else does. Imagine that, huh?" He turned and moved back to the door and she stopped him. "You want to know anything about what the police did, go and talk to the mayor. Luke Emerson said he'd make time for you if you wanted, but not until tomorrow. I guess you're just shit out of luck on all kinds of things today."

His laughter made her want to murder him. She'd even taken a step in his direction when she saw a man leaning against the building like he knew just what she was thinking. When he moved toward her, slowly, like a man with a purpose, Kimberly felt the hair on her arm dance and fear race down her back.

"You should be afraid." Nodding, she stared at the man. "You don't know me, but I'm going to be getting to know you very well. I'm going to be turning up just when you think you've hidden deep enough. Then when you are at the last of your patience with me, I'm going to show you what I do to humans that fuck with my family."

"Who are you?" He grinned, his mouth full of the sharpest teeth that she'd ever seen. She had to swallow twice before she could speak again. "No, you're wrong. I didn't do anything to your kind. I don't even...just stay away from me."

"Oh no, what fun would that be?" He laughed at her when she lifted her cane. He took it and broke it over his knee. "Be warned, Kimberly Schroeder. I'm Steward Thomas, and the

Emersons are mine to protect." Then he was gone.

By the time Kimberly got home, she was exhausted. She'd had to walk the entire distance because she'd had no money on her and no cell phone to call for someone to come for her. There had never been a use for it, as everyone did what she wanted when she wanted it. But she did map out her plans as she walked, and with every step she took, her plans for her grandniece and her daughter were harsher and harsher. And when she was finished with them, people were going to regret messing with her. Especially her niece.

Going into her home, the front door slightly opened, she nearly called out to Daniel. But the woman standing there had her thinking that things might be going her way after all. Hanging up her coat and putting the file on the table near the front door, Kimberly ignored her. She was trying to get her thoughts in order when Kimber finally spoke.

~~~

"You should be aware of a few things before I leave." Her aunt asked her why she thought she was going to be leaving at all. "Because you no longer have a hold over me. Not a single one. And I've been made aware of a few things since I've come home. Would you like to join us in the parlor?"

"You do not deem to tell me where we shall talk, young lady. This is still my house and I run—"

"No, it's not. It's mine." Kimber watched her face and knew that what she'd been told about her aunt and what she'd done had been true. Buying herself some time because the pain nearly took her to her knees, Kimber moved to the parlor. When Lee stood up with Luke and Hunter, she shook her head at them. She just needed a moment, that was all.

"What is the meaning of this? You cannot come in here

and state…. Who are these people and what are they doing in my home? And if you say that lie again, I shall hurt you, Kimber. I've had a terrible day and I'm not in the mood for you acting up." Her aunt looked at the three men that had come with her today. "Get out. My grandniece and I have a great many things to discuss, and I do not want my privacy invaded by the likes of you."

"This is my husband, Lee Emerson. His brothers, Luke, who I think you know, and Hunter. Cash, their father, is going to be here soon. He's watching my daughter." Her aunt huffed and sat down. "I heard about your day. And so you know, it's not going to be any better when I'm finished with you. Tate is a nice man and you treated him horribly. But I don't know why that should surprise me. You treat everyone that way, don't you?"

"I have no idea what you're going on about. You're going to stop this nonsense this moment. Tell these men to get out of my house and I'll tell you what you're going to do. I have your room prepared for you and contracts drawn up. You'll not be leaving here again until I think you are fit. This entire ordeal has taken a toll on you, and you'll be under my care. And don't think I've not made plans for that brat of yours. She is the first thing we're going to take care of. Her grandparents are going to take her from you as soon as they get here." Kimber laughed. "You think this is funny? It's not. I don't want you here anymore than you want to be here, but it is a necessity that I care for you."

"Yes, I heard. The same way you did my mother, no doubt. We found her will. But Hannah is staying with me. I've had a long…well, my new attorney has had a long talk with her grandparents. They are just tickled pink to know that a part of their son lives in my daughter. You should be very careful who you lie to, Kimberly. Things could and will come back to bite you in the ass big time." Kimber sat down and looked at her aunt. "My mother's will, it says a great deal more than what you said it did when she died. You lied to me, and everyone else, about it, didn't you?"

"I did no such thing. I protected you." Kimber asked her from what. "Men like this one that would take you for a ride then leave you with a baby in your belly. And don't think I don't know about your bogus marriage to him. You'll not marry anyone until I say you can. And even then he will be someone I pick, not you. Your choice in men is rather bad, don't you think? I'm having someone look into this supposed marriage even now. What did you think was going to happen, Kimber? That I'd simply let it go? I'm going to ruin you if you don't do as I say."

"I think you've ruined enough lives. Mine too if I hadn't figured out, with the help of my family, what kind of person you are. Not to say that I didn't have a hint of the monster you are, but they helped bring it to the surface." Her aunt picked up a small bell that Kimber had noticed were all through the house. Daniel, the butler, had told her that they were never to be moved and what they were used for. "They're not coming to help you. I've terminated them all. Daniel sobbed like a little boy. He said that he loved you. But the cook, she was so glad to know that you are no longer living here that she begged me to keep her on."

"What do you think you're doing? You have no rights that I don't let you have. And I have never...what do you want? Money? I have plenty." Luke cleared his throat then, and they all turned to him. "What is it you think you can add to this conversation? Nothing. There is not one thing you can say that anyone wants to hear. And I'm going to make sure that the townspeople know what sort of person you are. A wolf in my offices. Unheard of."

"Not as unheard of as you might think. And I'm pretty sure that most of the town knows what I am anyway. If you remember, recently we had the other mayor tossed out on his ass, and he's singing all about you and him and your little duties you had him perform. Not to mention, he kept all kinds of records about your dealings. Who would have thought you had that much power over such an idiot? But anyway, you have a lot to answer for, Kimberly. A great deal." Luke winked at Kimber before continuing. "As for money? You don't have any. Not even enough to get you to a decent hotel should you make it that far. So you know, you won't. When you leave here, we have a nice cell for you to stay in. Everything, including this house and all the things in it, belong to Kimber. And in case you get any bright ideas, which under the circumstances is funny since you've been short on bright ideas, the accounts have all been frozen, as have any assets that you have acquired with Kimber's money. That would include the house in France that you used to spy on your niece while she was there, as well as the restaurant that she worked at while trying her best to make a living. Shame on you for that."

That had hurt Kimber the most. Knowing that her aunt had made it so that she would fail. Her wages were cut, insurance was never within her reach, and she'd had to live in such squander, when her aunt had been living it up on her money. Not that Kimber wanted a great deal, but enough to have been able to make Hannah's life better would have been wonderful. While Luke went over the list of things that she owned, Kimber got up and made her way to the front hall. Men were there, agents from so many different groups that she had no idea where they were each from. They were there to arrest her aunt and take her away.

"Mrs. Emerson, are you all right?" She nodded, then shook her head. Lee came up from behind her and wrapped his arms around her. The man who had spoken to her seemed to understand that she was in need of somewhere quiet. "We have taken care of the sitting room should you like to go in there and rest. This won't be much longer."

Taken care of the sitting room. He'd made it sound like they'd scrubbed the carpets or something, when what they were really doing was inventorying everything. Not just the paintings on the wall, but the furniture as well. There were rugs on the floor that were worth more than she'd made in a year as a chef, she'd been told, and even the heavy drapes were worth thousands, but no less ugly for their worth. Lee led her into the room.

Tags were stuck on everything, even the lamps that she'd loved. A built-in cabinet housed hundreds of little tea cups and saucers, things that she knew her mother had loved. Going to that now, she opened the cabinet and pulled out the first one she saw.

It was small, fitting in the palm of her hand with plenty of room left over. The roses painted on it were so perfect they looked as if you could simply pick them off the cup and smell their dark heady scent. Putting it back before she gave in to her urge to toss it against the wall, she looked at Lee.

"I'm a mess." He didn't say anything, for which she was grateful. "This is...it's like a nightmare that I don't think I'll ever wake from. How could she do this things to me, to all of those people that she hurt? And I don't think she cared that she did them. Nor do I only believe part of what Luke has told me. She's simply the nastiest, meanest person ever to live."

"I'll agree with you there. But she's done this because she has always thought herself above everyone else." He leaned against the back of the couch that was covered in a thick material that made her think of paintings in a museum. Like something that Picasso would have painted. "Did Sloan ever tell you about the time the two of them butted heads?"

"I'm sure that Sloan butts heads with a lot of people. She's very strong and usually right." She smiled at him. "What did my aunt do to piss her off?"

"You know that Sloan owned all this land before we moved here, right? I mean, everything. She still does, as a matter of fact, but that's not where I'm going. And when we moved here, we were blown away by how much she did for the pack that she never had anything to do with. That sort of pissed off Hunter, but that's a different story all together. Anyway, about a year or so before we got here, Sloan was having some issues with the mayor before Conklin. He was the mayor before Luke, so I guess three of them back now. Okay, so she was having issues and Burdock, that was his name, he goes to your aunt and tells her that she is to make Sloan leave him alone. I kid you not, he said that she had to leave him alone. Well, in a fit of what can only be described as stupid, Kimberly has this team come in to cut through Sloan's fortress and get her. I'm not sure if there was a plan for what they were going to do with her once they got her, but they showed up with full intentions of cutting into her gates."

"Aren't her gates electrified?" Lee nodded, laughing. "And wolves. I've seen them around the property. Did they really think they were going to get past those too?"

"It never got that far. They showed up in these two huge fucking semis and park ed right outside her gates. Sloan apparently knew they were there and hyped up the juice a little. But she did warn them via the PA that they were trespassing." She nodded, loving that he was having so much fun with this story. "This big fucking guy just starts up his cutter and heads toward the gates. Now…from here the story gets a little wonky. The rumor is that the man hit the cutting machine in his hand to the gate and it fried him instantly. But Sloan swears that he was there. He did put the cutter to the fence, but he couldn't get loose from it fast enough. And in the end, four other men, trying to pull him off the fence, were burned too. I guess it took them a month in the hospital before they could be released. Then the company just disappeared in the middle of the night. Sloan said she didn't buy it, but I think she did."

"Oh my. I don't think she'd be one to piss off." He shook his head and came toward her. "I'm not sure what we're doing."

"Doing?" Lee pulled her into his arms and started to nibble on her neck. "I can think of all kinds of things we could be doing. Like going back to our place and trying out our new bed. Then we could shower together after I make love to you. Hannah won't be home for a little while. We can test my theory that our room is just far enough away from hers so that you can scream if you wish."

"I can't make love to you in the middle of the day. I have…you have to stop now. I can't think when you do that." He laughed a little but didn't stop. His mouth was doing wondrous things to her, and then he turned her in his arms

118

and pressed her against the wall. "You're driving me nuts."

The door opened with a loud crash and Lee nearly tossed her to the floor. Hunter looked like the hounds of hell were after him, and Lee looked like he was going to take them on. But when Hunter started talking, it was all she could do to keep up with him.

"I have to go. We have to...right now. There's the water, she said. And I have to hurry. She said...what are you doing? We have to leave here now and you have to drive me." Lee nodded, as confused as she was. "She's in labor. Sloan is in labor right fucking now."

They were in the truck in no time and pulling out of the driveway. Luke had opted to drive himself after he collected what he could from her aunt. Kimber hugged him to her, thanking him for doing this for her. He said it was his pleasure and told her that he'd see her at the hospital. Kimber looked at Lee when Hunter started talking again.

"The baby isn't due for another two weeks. What if something is wrong? Do you think she'll be all right? Both of them?" Kimber started to tell him everything was going to be fine, but he started talking again. "We have the bed ready and stuff. It's mine and my brother's...I didn't get the toy chest put together. She'll hate me. And Sloan will too."

"You do know this could be a false alarm, don't you? I mean, I had three dry runs when I had Hannah. Of course, my water never broke." She nearly screamed when he took her hand in his and squeezed. "Hunter, you're hurting me."

He let her go, but she wasn't sure he was listening to anyone. "I think that we should adopt from now on. She's been so exhausted all the time, and cranky. I've not pointed that out to her again after the first time. Who knew that women could be so violent when they're breeding? I'm not allowed to...can't you make this thing go any faster?" Lee looked at Hunter, then back at the road before he snapped at him.

"I'm not getting us killed so you can be in the waiting room four seconds earlier. Just sit there and keep talking like a man who is possessed." Kimber was glad she was there with these two right now. It was like watching a tennis match of terrified men. "Christ, what is that woman doing? Turn already, I'm trying to get to the hospital." The horn was laid on as he rounded the woman and her car.

"I'm pretty sure that you should just calm down." Lee glared at her. "Or pull over and let me drive. I know how, and I'm not all nutty like you two are."

"We're not either." Kimber laughed at the two of them. Then as Lee started to pass the next car in front of him, she grabbed onto the seatbelt like it was going to save her. Lee glanced over at her when she told him to slow the fuck down. "I'm trying to get him to his wife."

"Dead? Because that's what I'm thinking is going to happen if you don't take a fucking breath and drive like you have sense." He slowed down, and she was all ready to thank him when he passed the next car in front of them like he was racing across the finish line. "Lee, damn it, I'd like to be able to say yes if you ever get around to marrying me like all the paperwork already says."

"You'll marry me?" The car swerved when he looked at her and she growled. "You do that well, almost like you're a wolf already. I hope that you'll let me change you too. It'll be hard, but...hang on."

The turn in the front of the hospital was made on two wheels, she just knew it. And when he slid into one of the few parking spaces, she had to sit still in order to get her body under control. Hunter was out and running to the front of the hospital when she turned to Lee.

"You idiot. You could have gotten us all killed with that driving. Are you insane? What would Sloan have done to you if you would have gotten—?"

Lee got out of the truck and she wanted to find a gun and shoot him. But when he pulled her to him, her feet hanging out the door, she nearly kicked him when he dropped to one knee. He held out a ring to her as he smiled up at her.

"I love you. And so you know, I love Hannah as well. I have her a ring too. I wanted to ask you both to marry me, but since I nearly killed you to get you to agree, I thought I'd do this before you changed your mind. I love you with all my heart." He took her hand in his and slipped the ring on her finger. "I've done some things in my life that I'm not terribly proud of. Other things not as bad, but things that I wish I could do over and fix some of them. But having you in my life, you and Hannah, will be the best thing—no, the greatest thing—that has ever or will ever happen to me. And I'd very much like for you to be my wife, really my wife, so that I can show you every day how much I have come to love and admire you."

"Oh, Lee." She looked at the ring, then at him. "You do know that this changes nothing about the way you drove here and how pissed I am about it." He nodded. "Then yes, I'll marry you."

He jerked her from the seat and pressed her to the car, just as Hunter yelled from the doors for them to get their asses in there. Lee kissed her on the mouth quickly, then put her down. As they were moving to the door, he told her he was going to murder Hunter in his sleep the next time he stayed over. Kimber thought she might help him.

CHAPTER 9

Kimberly sat in the chair. She'd been taken out of her home in cuffs like she'd been a common criminal. And the worst part was, no one had bothered to tell her what she'd done that was so heinous. There were some things that she'd been told, but none of them, as far as she could see, were enough to have her taken to the police station as she'd been. But she would find out or heads were going to roll. When the man that had told her to have a seat sat across from her, she asked him if she could have her cane back. The one that she'd carried for the last ten years had been broken, of course, but she had a supply of them to use. He was shaking his head before she could explain to him that she needed it. Not to walk, but to use should the need arise.

"No. We're running some tests on it. There was blood splatter on it, and we're seeing who it might belong to. I don't suppose you'd tell me, would you? And I'm going to make you aware that the ones that we found in your possession in the house are being tested as well." She asked him why. "You mean aside from the blood? We have been notified that you've used them as weapons. We're looking for DNA. There are two unexplained deaths, and we think you might have had something to do with them."

"I have no idea what you're talking about." He asked her again if she wanted an attorney. "I have done nothing wrong that I would need one. I have very little use for them generally, and as soon as I'm freed from this…this place, I'm going to look into suing you and this department. You have no cause whatsoever to treat me this way. I'm Lady Kimberly Leta Schroeder, and I demand again that you allow me to leave here."

"You're not going anywhere until I say you can go. And for that matter, I want you to know that you have nowhere to go anyway. The house that you were occupying has been…. Are you sure you don't want a lawyer? If you can't afford one then we can—"

Kimberly slammed her hands down on the table before speaking. The man looked shocked, which was just what she'd been hoping for.

"I can afford it all, young man. And I have said to you twice now, I do not need an attorney. I have done nothing wrong but protect my interests. If that's a crime then I don't want to live in a country that would think so. In fact, I'm thinking of selling everything and moving to my home in France. I'll be taking my grandniece with me as soon as she rids herself of that brat. I will not have that thing in my home." Kimberly thought of all the things she was going to do to Kimber when she had her alone. First and foremost, she was going to beat her for putting her through this. "Kimber? Where is she? I want her here with me now. She has it in her head that she can treat me like something that has stuck to the bottom of her shoe. Well, I won't allow it. What I say is law."

"You think you're above such things as rules and regulations that other people have to follow, don't you? You really believe that everyone should do as you say just because of who, or in this case what, you think you are. I mean, you think that everyone — and I'm assuming me too — that we should just do as you say and damn the consequences." She said nothing, sensing a trap. It was just what she thought and knew to be fact, but he acted like he knew more than her, which was not even close to being possible. "What can you tell me about James Walden?"

"What about him? He was the father of the brat my grandniece thinks to have brought into my home. Not that she will, but she can think that all she wants. Having her there for those three days was bad enough. I will not have my life disrupted for a thing like that." She wondered what all this had to do with her being taken from her home. Kimberly rattled the chains at her wrists and glared at him. "I want you to release me from these shackles right now. I'm not an animal, and I do not appreciate you treating me like one."

"You're fine the way you are. I'm not finished with you as yet, and you being chained up makes it so I don't have to fight with you as well." When she started to tell him it wasn't a request, he leaned back in his chair. "You're going to go down for the murder of Walden and a few other people. Did you know that? I really wish there was more, but that's all we have on you for now."

"Go down? Whatever do you mean? I told you, release

me before I have to find someone that will." When he didn't move, she started to stand. But the chains held her so that she had to stoop over. Sitting down, she glared at him. "What is your name? When I'm let out of here, and that will be soon, I'm going to have you fired. You're making me very mad right now. I'm not a very nice person when I'm upset. You should ask my grandniece what it is to upset me."

Kimberly had been the one to deal out punishment since she was a child. No one around her would do as she said until she showed them what it was to upset her. When it was clear to her that someone was going against her wishes, Kimberly would show them not only the error of their ways, but also give them a constant reminder of what it was to turn against her. Kimberly demanded again to be released or else.

"You'll get over it. You never answered me about Walden. What do you know about his death?" He looked as if he had all day to wait for her to answer him. "We have notes on conversations that you had with your grandniece, as well as a conversation that you had with her in person. She paints a very disturbing picture of you and your ways of dealing with someone."

Kimberly had had enough of this. "He's dead, that's what I know. What knowledge should I have concerning him or the fact that he is no longer a problem? Had he done what he was told, then none of this would be necessary. You have put thoughts into Kimber's head, and now she thinks to have me brought here under the guise of telling people our business. I don't care what has happened to that man. Good riddance to him is all I have to say about that." The man was getting on her last nerve. Slamming her hands down on the table got her no reaction at all. "You are to release me this moment or I shall have to call in some help. And when I do, there will be trouble as you have never seen before."

"Like the trouble you gave Kimber?" She asked him what he meant. "You didn't have her life made harder when she was trying to raise her daughter? Have her fired from her job? Take half her wages when she could have used them for a better life for them both? Or the fact that you had a man dating her that had no reason whatsoever to do so until you paid him?"

"Of course I did those things to her. She is my ward. And regardless of what you say about her age, she is mine to do with as I see fit. As for Walden? It's what she needed done to bring her back to where I demanded her to be in the beginning. This was her mother's fault. I forbade her to let her go, and not only did she let her go when I said not to, but she told her not to come home even if she was to die. That ruined all my plans. Once she was home for the funeral, she would never have left. I would have made sure of that." He asked her what sort of plans. "Her place is with me. Catering to my needs and what I want. Not out doing things that would…well, get her with a brat. That thing will have to go too. I do not have the time, nor do I have the need, to have something like that in my home. Children have no good use other than to make them do as you please. That one is too mouthy already, and I will take care that she's not in my life once you have let me go. As I have asked you to do several times now. I demand that you set me free of these chains. I've done nothing to warrant you treating me like I'm a criminal."

"You don't think you've done anything wrong? I mean, you don't think it was wrong in having your grandniece think that she's a failure? Or to—?"

"She is a failure. What do you think I've been trying to tell you?" Kimberly held her temper as best she could, because to lose it now would only hurt herself. Each time she pulled against the shackles at her wrist, it was painful. "She's done things...terrible things. Lying with that man. I told him he was only to make her think that he was in love with her, bring her here, and I would take care of the rest. And then I find out months later, too late to have anything done about it, that he has filled her belly with a brat. You have no idea how that ruined my plans for her. Nor do you understand the work I had to do to change things around to fix even the smallest of things."

"So you had him killed." She said nothing. Of course she had. It wasn't as if he'd not brought it on himself. "Miss Schroeder, why don't you tell me your plans for Kimber? What kind of things has she ruined for you?"

"Everything. How am I to control her when she will not listen to a single thing I've told her to do? I brought her here, did I not? And that child. She was to do as I told her." The man said that she'd said that, but what was she to have done? "The will and money, of course. How am I to control it if she isn't here to turn it over to me? Why my brother left it to her mother is beyond me. She would have just flittered it away. And she did too. Giving it to Kimber to waste her time on that schooling. What for, I ask you? She wasn't going to be a domestic. And she certainly isn't going to be a wife to some man. I'm going to make sure of that too."

"You're a bit too late for that, I'm afraid. She is married. To Lee Emerson. They seem like a really happy couple, and Cash thinks the world of her and that little girl. But I'm guessing you don't approve of Lee." Kimberly only huffed at him.

"He's a good man. Holds a good job. From what I understand, he loves Kimber very much, and little Hannah. It wouldn't surprise me if he adopts the little tyke. And soon."

"He can have the child for all I care. As for him wedding Kimber, that isn't legal. She's my ward until I say differently. And I have certainly not given her permission to do anything of the kind. She will have to realize, and soon, that I'm law. When I speak, there will be consequences if she does not listen. She should have known that by now." Kimberly glared at the man again. "And you will as well. Take these things off of me this minute. I am well past telling you to do it and you sitting there like you have no intentions of letting me go."

"I don't. In fact, as stimulating as I find talking to you, I think it's all for nothing. You're too stubborn to realize that you're finished." She asked him what he was talking about. "I'm not letting you go. In a few hours some men are going to come in and ask you questions again. And when you give them the answers that you have me, they're going to cart your ass off to some funny farm, where you're going to spend the rest of your life. Because lady, you are one fucked up piece of work."

"You cannot talk to me this way. I'm Lady Kimberly Leta Schroeder, and I am the…where is Ben Conklin? Bring him to me this minute. He was the only man besides that sheriff that knew how to treat me. I had only to ask and give them a little money and they'd do everything I wanted. Bring him here now." When he didn't move to do her bidding, she slammed her hands down on the table again. "You are going to pay for this, young man. I am not a woman to be trifled with. Where is Ben? Answer me this instant."

"Prison, where you should be. And more than likely will

be once this goes to court. Luke Emerson, Kimber's brother-in-law, is the one you're going up against, so I'm thinking you should really choose your lawyer well. As for bringing Conklin to you? That's going to be a big fat no."

When he left her sitting there, Kimberly tried to think what she was supposed to do now. Things were not going to just do themselves, and she had projects in the works that she had to oversee. This was just not the way she had planned her day.

A few minutes later a woman came into the room with her and told her to stand up. When the chains were taken from the small ring in the table, Kimberly thought she was free, but the cuffs were put back on her almost immediately.

"Where are you taking me?" Nothing. The woman actually had the nerve to tell her to shut up. Kimberly was so shocked by it that she nearly missed what she said about the cell. "I'm not going to any holding cell. I've made it perfectly clear to everyone that I want to be freed. What are you doing? Take these things off me right this minute."

Two men were in the hall when she was brought out of the room. As she was shoved down the hallway toward the door, Kimberly thought of her grandniece. This was all her fault. She'd ruined her plans and now she was going to have to pay for it. The child, the brat, was going to be the thing that would bring her in line, so that was where she'd start. And the sooner the better.

When Kimberly was standing outside a cell with bars all around it, she turned to the woman who was holding her chains.

"You cannot think to make me sit in there." The woman, an officer of all things, just told her to go in and to shut up. "I think this farce has gone on long enough. Take these ridiculous things off me and I will not take measures into my own hands and have you fired. Do you have any idea who you are talking to? What kind of power I have because I have money?"

"You'll go in there on your own two feet or I get to toss your butt in there." Kimberly started to tell her that she would not when she saw the man behind her. The officer turned and looked at the man, then looked at Kimberly. The smile on her face did not look like things were going to go well for her. "He's here to talk to you. And I'm pretty sure that you're not going to like a thing he says to you. And so you know, he's not going to put up with your crap either."

"I don't want him to come near me. Take him away." Kimberly found herself in the cell and the door locking behind her. She hadn't even realized that the cuffs had been removed, she'd been so terrified of the man. When he walked to the door, she backed as far from him as she could, touching the wall to her back.

"You've been warned, have you not?" Nodding, she wondered how Steward had found her, here of all places. "I'm not in the best of moods, Kimberly. And to have to come here, during the day, to make sure that you are aware of what is going to happen to you does not make my mood or my ability to deal with you any easier. You are a pain in the ass."

"I demand that you leave me alone. I have no use for you or your kind." He laughed at her. "I've done not one thing to you. Not one. I've been living my life the way I want, and everyone here believes they can come in and intrude on my plans. I will not have it."

"Well, that's just too bad. And as for you not harming me? No, not me personally. But I did tell you to leave them alone, didn't I? The Emersons are more like family to me than anyone has ever been. And they have never asked for anything in return. You demand and demand, and then when that doesn't go your way, you hurt. Why is that?" Kimberly said nothing. "Answer me."

She knew what he was doing. Using his mind tricks on her. Kimberly wanted to say that it didn't affect her, but she knew that it wasn't anything she could control. Nor was it anything that she could buy. To have such power over someone would be a wondrous thing. But when he demanded that she answer him again, she had no choice in the matter.

"I have no idea what you want to know. I should have the things that I want and in the way that I want them. Why anyone else would want things their way is beyond me. It's the way things should be for the good of those around me, and everyone should simply give it to me or do what I say. How am I supposed to make sure that things are done the way I want them if people are forever thinking their way is the better way? I am Lady Kimberly Leta Schroeder, and I will have it go according to my plans or there will be trouble, mark my words." He laughed. A loud boisterous laugh that had people turning their heads to look at them. "Stop that. You're making people stare at us. I do not want anyone to know that I have been detained. It's bad enough that I've had to waste time here that I should be spending at home, but Kimber will soon know that she was wrong in even trying this."

"Detained? I'm thinking you're more than detained, Kimberly. You're here for the duration." He snapped his fingers, and a chair appeared behind him. As he sat down, she wondered what else he could make appear, and he grinned. "I will not let you go, so don't even bother demanding anything of me. I won't lift a finger to do a thing for you…not now, nor in any foreseeable future, if you have much of a future. I like you just where you are."

"I did nothing wrong. As soon as I'm out of here, people are going to pay for this. You mark my words. I should not be treated this way." He asked her why. "Because I am Lady—"

"Fuck that shit. You aren't lady anything. And you've never been further than the United States, no matter what little stories you make up. You gave yourself that title when someone snubbed you at a party once you returned from that little stay you had to endure when you tried to hit that cop. That didn't go over well for you either, did it?" Kimberly shook her head. "Sit down and shut up. I don't have a great deal of time right now, and you're lucky that I don't just kill you to end this shit. As I have pointed out, I am not in the best of moods."

"You can't kill me. I'm not going to allow it. I know my rights and I'm not allowing you to do any such thing." He laughed again. "I demand to know why you think that I should be here. Then I want you to get me out of here. I'm not in a very good mood either."

"You killed James Walden for one. And the family that was having lunch in the same café when the man drove up on the walkway to get to him. Oh, you didn't cause the accident that took their lives, but you paid a man to do it for you. Yes, you were not involved in those murders or the two after, but when you pay someone to do the killing for you, you are just as guilty. You might not think so, but the law is very clear on that."

Kimberly knew all this.

"So? They were only a casualty of what was needed for

me to have my plans put into motion. Had Kimber been with him, as she should have been, then I would not have to work so hard to get her to come to heel. Everyone that was involved was paid. And as much as I hated to do it, I have made sure that the driver of that car was well paid for his part in this as well." She smiled then. "And that brat wouldn't have been born either had the two of them been killed. Do you have any idea how much that thing has ruined things for me? Just a simple thing, that's all he had to do, but Kimber had stayed home with a sick head. She is ruining my plans every time she takes a breath."

"Good for her. More people should ruin your plans. There would be less death surrounding you when you go to trial. Oh, and then there is the husband of your niece. That was very bad of you, Kimberly. The man was only asserting his rights as the husband of a very wealthy woman." Kimberly only nodded now. She had no idea where he was going with rehashing things that she knew about. "What did you do to him? Or should I say, what did you do to the two of them?"

"Camden was a problem from the start. You should have seen him. Trying to get my Leta to do his bidding instead of mine. What did he think was going to happen when he told me that he was moving me out of my own home and I was never to return? Did he really expect me to simply wish him well? Then he said he was taking over the running of her companies. They were my companies. I had built them up. My father should have left them to me, not some sniveling halfwit that had no more idea what to do than a brat would." Kimberly thought of the man that she'd come to despise. "I had no idea they were even seeing each other. Leta was leaving my house and running off with that man nightly. Then when she was caught with him she told me that they were married. Married. Like that was something special."

"It was to them." Kimberly snorted. "So what did you do to him? Then her? I heard that you had her put in a home across the country after her husband was dead. She was a grieving young woman, and you shipped her away like she was nothing more than day old trash. But that didn't work out so well either, did it?"

"No it did not, and you well know it. But he had to go. What more is there to say on that? You would have done the same if he had come into your home demanding things his way. Then after I sent her away, hoping that while she was there they'd do something, anything about her state of mind, they informed me that she was with child. A child? What was I to do with a brat? And no matter how much I offered, they refused to have it aborted. Said that she was too far along and that it might kill her. So? One less thing for me to have to contend with. As if they had any say in that whatsoever. So she came here with a babe in her arms and an attitude that bordered on insolence. And no matter what, that child never left her side." Smiling, she thought of Camden's last moments. "That fall from the stairs, however, was very well planned. It was a lovely sight to see. Sometimes I go back up to the place and think of him tumbling over and over down the stairs."

"So you pushed him down the stairs." Kimberly shook her head but smiled. This was a fun game, having someone try to figure out all her plans. "But you did have something to do with it."

"Absolutely not. I did loosen the rug just a little, and if he tripped over it, I had nothing to do with it." Kimberly looked at the vampire in front of her. "I'm sure that you've done worse than what these people here think to accuse me of. I'm just a woman trying to get ahead in the world. And to make sure that things are just the way they should be for me. What is the harm in that? None. I will rule my own house, not some upstart that thought that he knew more than I did in the running of my money."

He stood up and so did she. Kimberly might have enjoyed talking to him for a little while, but he was still a monster and she didn't trust him. She actually trusted no one but herself.

"The difference between the two of us is that while I have done things I'm not proud of, I've never fucked over one of my family. Nor, and this is where you have screwed up big time, have I been caught." Steward stepped back and pointed to the camera that hung pointed at the two of them. His smile, one that showed all his teeth, made her cringe back again in fear, a feeling that she was as unfamiliar with as she was saying she was sorry for something that she'd done. Not that she ever apologized for anything she did or said. "And, unlike you, I'm not going to prison for it. Goodbye, Kimberly. May you rot in hell."

Kimberly stood there for several minutes after he'd gone, trying to work out what this all meant. What had he meant, prison? She wasn't going anywhere but home. Moving to the front of her cell, she yelled for someone to come to her now. As they all moved around the room, some of them sitting at their desks, others just talking on the phone, she saw Kimber coming toward her. And with her, the young man from this morning.

"It's about time. Come have them unlock this door and take me home. You and I have a great deal to discuss, and for once you are going to obey me. I've had a terrible day and I'm in a sour mood. Unlock this door and let's begin." Kimberly stepped back and watched for one of them to do her bidding. "What are you waiting for? You heard me. Get me out of here and then take me home. I don't know what you were thinking, but I will not stand for this kind of treatment again. This is no way for you to treat me after all that I've put up with from you."

"I'm afraid you'll have to get used to it. And as for the things you've done for me, I think you should say the things you've done to me. And there has been a great deal, hasn't there, Kimberly? But I'm only here to tell you goodbye and good riddance." Kimberly started to ask Kimber what she was talking about when she continued. "We found Mother's will. We also found the paperwork on the house, as well as your notes on the former mayor and police chief."

"You were snooping in my things? How dare you. You are to bring my things back to me this minute. I will not stand for this, Kimber. You have gotten on my last nerve of late, and I'm finished with trying to be nice to you. You'll do as—"

"You were being nice to me? When? I'd very much like to know one time when you were nice to me." Kimberly glared at the man when he laughed. "I asked you a question, Kimberly. When did you think you were nice to me? Because not once in all my life have I a single memory of you being anything but the mean person you are today."

"You'll call me by my proper title or nothing at all. And you're not dead, are you? Believe me when I tell you, it was not for lack of trying on my part." The moment the words left her mouth, she looked around the room. She'd been loud, but it was Kimber's fault. She'd been a bad seed from the beginning, and now she was trying to make her say things that she shouldn't. "Get me out of here and I'll talk to you. I cannot believe that you've taken this thing between us this far. I'm in charge, Kimber, and the sooner you realize that, the better things are going to go for you."

"You and I are finished. I will not come to see you again. I won't listen to your lies, and I will not have you around me ever again. You are nothing but a hateful, mean woman who wants things her way, and damn what other people might want or need." Kimberly nodded. "You actually believe that, don't you? That you should have everything your way simply because you want it."

"Yes." Kimberly frowned. "And why shouldn't it be? I'm the one that has had to work and plan things to come out the way they have. Do you think that had your mother been left in charge things would have gone well? No, they would not have. And your grandfather, my own father, he was a fool and would have given every penny to anyone that asked for it. Mother was no better. They had to be dealt with or I'd be nothing but a pauper by now. And this is how you repay me? By treating me like I'm nothing?"

"No, how I'm going to repay you is this. I'm going to take all the money that you have, and I do thank you for that, and give it to my daughter and any other children that I have. They can do with it what they want. They can spend it on coloring books and crayons if they wish, or go to college with it. I don't care. And when it's all gone I'm going to dance a jig. Because that money has done nothing for me but cause me heartache and pain. And you, Kimberly, are not going to be able to do shit about it."

"You'll do nothing of the sort. That is mine, all of it. I worked harder than anyone in making it work for me, and you'll not give it to that brat. Or any other monsters that you have with this thing. Get me out of here, Kimber. Right now." Kimberly watched the two of them walk away. They were actually going to leave her here. "Kimber, come back here now. You hear me? I said to come here now and have them let me go. I have things I must see to."

She stood there for another ten minutes. She knew it had been that long because she could see the clock on the wall near the doors. No one bothered to come to let her out, nor did anyone come to see if she needed anything. And she needed plenty. Sitting back down again, she sat there and tried to think what she'd done to deserve this. What had she done to Kimber that would make her think she could treat her, Lady Kimberly Leta Schroeder, this way?

"She's an ungrateful brat is what she is." Leaning back on the cot, she sat there for several more minutes, trying her best to figure out what had gone wrong with the world. First there were her parents, then her own niece, and now this. The entire lot of them was going to pay when she was out of this place. And she knew just who to get to do it too.

Ben Conklin was a man to get things done. She'd liked the man. A great deal. He could bend and scrape when she needed him to, and the two of them had made a great deal of money. Her more than him, but he'd been a good ally to have. Along with the sheriff. Sheriff Barker had been helpful at getting rid of bodies, too, should it come to that.

The longer Kimberly sat there, the more she realized that no one was coming for her. And not only that, no one here cared. As her meal was brought to her and no one would change it out for something more palatable, she came to realize something else. There wasn't going to be any help from any of them. If things were going to happen, she'd have to make them happen for herself, just as she normally had to.

When the room darkened, she laid her head on the inadequate pillow and tried to think what she had to do to get out of here. While nothing was coming to mind, plenty of plans about what she was going to do when she finally left did. Kimber was going to have to be taught a lesson. She'd thought about simply having her killed, but that would require more time than she had. Finding someone to do it, having to work out a payment arrangement. Then there was the simple fact that as long as she was free and walking around, it was going to continue to be a problem. No, Kimber had to be killed.

Lee

CHAPTER 10

Kimber sat and watched Sloan sleep. She'd been here about five minutes, not much longer than that, but Sloan had been sleeping soundly since she'd arrived. The baby was asleep too, and her little face was all she could see of the little bundle. Kimber wanted to pick her up in the worst kind of way.

"You can, you know." Kimber looked at Sloan, who was staring at her with the most serene smile. "I just like holding her close to me and smelling that wonderful baby smell. Just hold her. I know you want to."

"I do." Kimber put her bag on the floor with the brightly colored gift bag beside it. As she stood up and walked to the bassinet, she continued talking to Sloan. "Hannah and I went shopping yesterday after we left the jail. I left the tags on things in case you get the same things we did. But we had so much fun."

"How did that go with your aunt? I'm assuming not so well." Kimber only shook her head. "Yeah, that sucks. I remember when my guardian came to my house once and told me that I had crippled him in his pursuit of a normal life. Then he tried to kill me. Sucks to have family that you'd just as soon not. But what can you do?"

"She's acting like we're doing her a great disservice by treating her this way. And everything she's done to us, it has been because she wanted it and no other reason that I can see. Steward saw her before we did. He said that while she's insane, she really believes that what she's done is all right. And that anyone that disagrees with her should be put to death. Not his words, but that's what I took from it." Kimber sat down and held the little girl tightly in her arms. "I can hardly remember when Hannah was this tiny. She was all I had left of her dad. He was dead by then."

"She's something else, your daughter. When she was with me the other day, she informed me that she was going to be my niece as well. I told her I was fine with that, but that I would require a few things. The little minx told me so long as it was reasonable and sound, it was fine by her. I nearly wet myself laughing so hard." Kimber nodded as she peeled some of the blankets from the baby in her arms. "Do you and Lee want children?"

"I think he does. He's mentioned it, but nothing concrete as yet." Kimber looked at Sloan. "I needed to talk to you about something. I started to ask Addie, but she kinda scares me a little, and Jack simply scares the shit out of me with her laid back, I can kill you sort of ways. I don't think she will, but she still frightens me. And, of course, Hannah thinks she's wonderful."

"Yeah, that's Jack for you. Who would have thought that only a few months ago she was this timid little thing with not a lick of confidence? Something like me, I guess. As you know, as your alpha I can only advise you on things. I won't make you do them." Kimber was glad that she'd gotten more information on pack things before coming here. She knew what Sloan and Hunter could make her do and some of the things that she could demand of them. Not that she would, but it was nice to know that she had things on her side as well. Sloan laughed before continuing. "However, as your sister-in-law, I can give you anything you want so long as it's reasonable and sound." They both laughed, startling the little girl to look up at her and glared. In that moment Kimber knew that this little girl was going to be a great person, just like her parents.

"You're opening a restaurant in town. I'd like to help you. Not help you so much as be a part of it." Sloan nodded but said nothing. Kimber looked at the baby rather than Sloan as she continued. She didn't want to see the disappointment on Sloan's face right now. "I'm figuring that you'll have some sort of cook off to find a chef. I was fired from my last job because…well, that's not really important, but I'm really good at…I'd really like to have the chance to try out."

"Kimber, look at me." She did, and Kimber could see the hint of a smile, but she had no idea what to make of it. "You're the one that I was hoping would run it. I don't know a great deal about the kitchen other than what I can do to help out my family. I wouldn't have any idea how to make sure that everyone sitting at my table got what they wanted, how they wanted it, in a reasonable, timely manner. I can cook, don't get me wrong, but not like you can. Not nearly on that scale."

"I thought you'd want Lee to run it. I mean, he'd be my pick. Since we've been living together, he's made us some fantastic meals. He said that he doesn't want to be the chef for it, but I'm not sure." Sloan told her that Lee didn't want it. "Why not? I mean, really, why doesn't he want to have his own restaurant?"

"He likes helping them long term. When he goes into a place that is failing or nearly so, he told me that he enjoys bringing it back if it's fixable. He hates to tell them it's not going to work, and believe me, he's gotten really good at knowing too, but he enjoys the uphill battle that comes with bringing something to life again. And while he does like to cook and enjoys it, it's the end project that he likes more than that."

"He told me about the same thing." Kimber ran her fingers down the soft downy cheek of the baby in her arms. "I'm terrified of being in his family. In this family. I'm not sure I know what to do with you guys. I know that sounds silly, but you're so nice to each other and help out when you need to."

"Why shouldn't we help each other?" Kimber stood up and took the baby to her mom. But when she started to pull back, Sloan put her hand on her arm. "Why are you afraid of this family?"

"I'm afraid that having Kimberly as my aunt will make it so you guys won't accept us. I'm not afraid of the family. It's being a part of one. This one. I've had so many fuck ups in my life. One right after the other. And this thing with my aunt? Christ, I had no idea of the stuff that she'd been up to. The Feds said that we can do what we want with the house, but they're still going over some of the things inside it. Did you know that she had a Rembrandt? No one can figure out where she might have acquired it. And it was in her closet with some old shoes that they think she was tossing out." Kimber sat down again. "Anyway, Clemmie has asked me if she could buy the house if we're not going to live in it. I told her that I had to wait and see what...Lee said that I'd have to clear it with you and Hunter first."

"You do. I know what she has in mind for the house, and I think it's a wonderful idea. But I'd not sell it to her. Not yet at any rate. Rent it to her. Not for much, a few hundred a month, just enough to cover the cost of running it. Renting it will save both of you so much in revenue, as well as it's a nice tax write-off for you." Kimber nodded. Luke had told her that as well. "What is it, Kimber? I can't help you if you don't tell me."

Kimber laughed. "Where do I even begin? Let's see. Hannah's grandparents want to come here and see her. And they are still worried, or so Addie has told me, that they'll have to take her from me. They don't want custody of her, not this late in their lives, but they don't want a drug addict raising their son's child either. That's what my aunt told them I was, a person who was high all the time, and when I wasn't high, I was fucking anything, and I mean anything, with a dick. Then there are the things with my aunt, which I know you're aware of. The money that was found in the house notwithstanding, I'm now fairly well off. I have no idea how to be anything but dirt poor and struggling. But Lee has told me that even without her money, we're well off. I have no idea what that means, but he's pretty confident. Hannah wants to change her name to Emerson. Like now. And she is so in love with Cash...well, so am I. But she wants him to come and live with us forever. I'm sure that he likes her as well, but now that he has his own granddaughter, I'm worried that she'll be hurt.

It's not him, I just worry because of...I'm overthinking this, I know, but I'm very stressed right now."

"You are. But let's work through this. Cash. He's the most loving and understanding man I've ever met, including my husband. The first man that I ever trusted too. As for your daughter, he's already making plans for her birthday, which I understand is soon. And just the other day, I heard him call both her and Kelly his family, and was showing off pictures of all of them to Mabel. Who I'm sure is sick of seeing them." Kimber nodded, knowing that the man had taken more pictures of her daughter in the last few days than Kimber had Hannah's entire life. Sloan laughed again. "Well off, Lee told you? Well, you are that. Very well off. Lee has not spent a great deal of his money, and I pay him very well. The house that the three of you live in is paid for. He has invested well and owns three more properties across the world. All paid for. He's worth millions last I had him in my office, and he'll be worth more before the end of the year. He's that good."

"I never expected that much. I mean, a lot, but...millions? What does he do to...? Never mind. I was thinking down a path I no longer have to. But my aunt. She'll continue to make problems for us. She's not going to just go away." Sloan leaned back on the bed and started nursing the baby. "I'm not even sure what all she's done to how many people, but I'm betting that there is a lot."

"There is. Addie told me. Do you want to know?" Kimber shook her head. "Good. That's the way to approach this. You don't owe her anything, and from what I've been told, you don't need it. Luke said that her prison sentences are going to be for a very long time, but at her age, it won't be long anyway. And everything that she has taken from you has been returned. Correct?"

"Yes. The money, if that's what you mean." Sloan told her it wasn't all of it, but some. "She's not…she never has seen what her actions can do to other people, and she just doesn't care either. I've never seen a person so set in her ways to the point of murdering people to have it that way. Why would she think the things she does? And for what reason? She had money, more than either of us could spend in several lifetimes. Why?"

"Who knows? Perhaps her parents or someone along the line gave her what she wanted, or not. That would make her a bully, I suppose. And that's what she is. A bully. But one with the means to back things up with money. That's not quite true about her not caring. She does care, but only in the way that it affects her. Steward talked to her, as you've said, and he's talked to Hunter and me as well. He doesn't think she's insane as much as self-absorbed. It's all about her and her gains, and hell hath no fury should things not go according to the gospel of Kimberly Schroeder." Sloan changed breasts, then continued. "But what I meant was, everything has been returned. I mean your reputation as a chef, as well as all the back money that you were owed. I heard that you put it in an account for Hannah. What a lovely idea. As smart as she is, she's going to need that for college, and sooner than you think."

"She's being tested for another grade level. They put her in the third grade when we arrived, but the teachers say that she's well above that. And I got a very nice letter from the board of review about my college scores too. Did you know that instead of being second in my class, I was first?" Sloan congratulated her. "Thank you. But Kimberly did that, had

147

them take away my points to make me second because she didn't want me to have the best. Not unless she approved. How sick is that?"

"You are well rid of her." Sloan adjusted her clothing and lay back with the baby on her shoulder. "You've never asked me what her name is. I thought for sure you would right off. No one has. I'm somewhat disappointed in that."

Kimber laughed. "I heard that we're not to ask until you're ready to explode with the news. I want to know. I really do." Sloan told her she was going to kill Jack. "How did you know…? Never mind, I would have guessed the same person. Did you know that when I first met her, she told me she was the nice one? Scared the shit out of me."

"I'd like to introduce you to Lea Alexandrea Bethany Emerson." Kimber told her it was beautiful. "The Lea is for my mom, who I never knew, and Alexandrea Bethany for Hunter's mom, who died before I met him. Cash has no idea either. I can't wait for him to find out. The old poop is going to love it. And he already does her and the rest of the kids."

After they looked over the things that she and Hannah had gotten the new baby and the gift that Kimber had gotten for Sloan, she told her that she had to go. Before she left, Sloan called her back.

"You're going to have to come up with a name for your restaurant, love. No pressure, but Jack is biting at the bit to get your stationary done, as well as the logo for it. And she's going to blast you across the airways until you have a waiting list for a table for ten years or more. I'd tell her to slow down on that when you talk to her. Easing into this slowly will be better for us all, I think." Kimber leaned against the door, suddenly overwhelmed again. "It needs to be simple and elegant. Something clean and full of promise."

"But no pressure, right?" Sloan laughed. "I'll give it some thought. But the first thing that comes into my head is just Emerson's. I have no idea why, but there you have it." Sloan told her that she loved it. "I'll think on it. But I love it too."

Kimber went back to the house feeling a little lighter. Nothing had been resolved really, but she did feel better. When she pulled into the long drive, she saw Lee's car and one that she didn't know. Getting out, she moved to the house only to be stopped when a man dressed in a coat and tails stepped in front of her from the shadows. Taking a step back from him, she nearly fell off the deck, and would have if Lee hadn't caught her.

"This is Steward Thomas. He's come to ask if we can put him up for a few days. Something has come up on his home and…well, he needs a place to rest." Kimber nodded. "Do you know what that means?"

"He's a vampire. And I'm assuming he needs somewhere safe." The man smiled at her and she saw his teeth. "Don't do that around my daughter or there will be hell to pay. I don't care what you are."

"She and I have met." Kimber started forward and he backed up with a laugh. "I have done nothing to her. She is… the two of you are a great deal alike. She warned me that I would not live long should I harm either of you. I like her. I'm assuming that I will like you both."

"I do too, and just the way she is." He nodded. "Why do you need a place to stay? I'm pretty sure that if something or someone makes you nervous, I don't want them to know that you're here."

"No. It's not that. I just need someplace to rest during the day. I have commissioned a house to be built. There is a place that I should like to stay, but there are too many Feds hanging around there." She asked him if he meant her aunt's house. "Yes. For me to live in her home, even for a night, would send her over the edge. Or I should say, more so. 'My kind,' as she calls us, is not welcome to be near her."

"She's not a nice person." He only nodded. "Stay there if you want. I'm not sure what there is in the way of accommodations, but you're welcome to stay. I'm not going to. The Feds, for the most part, have done what they need, so I don't think they'll be much of a bother."

"I have heard that you have plans for it?" This time she nodded. "I like the idea. I think I would very much enjoy seeing some local flair around here. I'm also to understand that you are going to be the new chef at the restaurant that Sloan is building. I think that's an excellent idea. I look forward to seeing it."

"But you don't eat." He nodded and smiled again. "You know, you're scaring me. Just...I don't know. Just try to keep your teeth in your mouth if you don't mind."

"I will from now on. I'm so used to...people are not as accepting as you and the Emersons have been. It's a rare thing to be a vampire and have a family welcome you with open arms. Especially wolves. We are, as you might have heard, mortal enemies. But here we are, the best of friends." They all turned when he did to look at the lone man coming across the yard from the wooded area. Steward turned to Lee as he spoke in a low voice. "Graham, is he any better?"

"Not really. I think his nightmares are affecting not just his sleep but his wellbeing as well." Steward nodded and looked at her as Lee continued. "He's moving into his own home next week, I guess. He bought Ellis's home not long ago, but had carpets put in rooms where Ellis had put nothing as yet. He is having it painted too. Ellis had left the walls a stark white. I think he's put in a work barn too. For his equipment."

"He is a good man. Maybe I'll have a talk with him. See if I can get him to rest easier."

As the two men walked off, Graham toward his car with Steward walking with him, Kimber looked at Lee. He was watching his brother closely, and she wondered if he was worried that Steward would harm him. But as soon as they entered the house, she didn't worry about anything else as he pressed her against the wall.

~~~

He needed her. Not just for sex, though that was wonderful, but her near him, her touching him as well. When Lee lifted her up in his arms and her legs wrapped around him, he moved his mouth to her shoulder and nipped none too gently at her throat.

"Take me." He growled low at her command and tore her blouse off. There was no one else in the house right now and he wanted her just as badly. Pulling her legs from around him, he stood her against the wall as he dropped to his knees.

"I'm going to have my fill of you, then the wolf is." She nodded and pulled her bra off. It was in shreds anyway, but he watched as she cupped her breasts and tugged at her nipples. "I'm going to eat you. Then I'm going to fuck you hard. After my wolf has had his fill."

"Do it, please. I'm so wet now that I'm soaking through my pants." He buried his nose in her pussy then inhaled deeply. "Please, Lee. I can't wait much longer."

Tearing her pants and panties off her left her standing in

only her shoes. He loved that she didn't wear stockings under her pants, but wanted to see her in the kind that only went to her thighs. He wanted to peel them off her slowly as he drank from her. As he licked the cream running down her thigh, Lee let his wolf take him.

He was more aggressive than he'd ever been. Nearly knocking her to the floor, he ate her pussy like he would his dinner. Not just lapping at her, bringing to her peak over and over, he actually nipped at her tender flesh until she screamed out his name. Lee told her to lay down, and his wolf barely let her move until she was spread out for them on the front carpet with her legs wide apart. His wolf lay down and began his feast again. Lee wanted her too, wanted to eat her, give her as much pleasure as his wolf was, but he simply wouldn't back off. When he stood up suddenly and lunged at her tender belly, Lee screamed at him to stop, but it was too late by then.

His wolf whimpered twice before he settled near her. When she cried out, trying to pull away from the teeth that were tearing into her, Lee spoke to her, trying to calm her down. But the more she struggled against his sharp mouth the more pain he was causing her, until Lee had no choice but to call out to Hunter. Lee was beyond terrified of what they had done, and he was also afraid that she might die.

I've hurt her. Badly. My wolf just tore into her belly without taking the time to prepare her. Hunter, I don't think it's going to work. He's going to kill her. Hunter said he was on his way, but he was at his house and may take a bit. *Bring...find Steward for me, please? I don't know if he can save her either, but her heart rate is so very slow right now. She's going to die. I can't lose her.*

I'm coming. I've contacted him. He said that he's close and should be there soon. Has he been in your house, Lee? Have you invited him in? He hadn't, and he told Hunter that while Steward had been at the house just now, he'd not gone in. *Then how will he get in to help you? I'm assuming that you're in your house and not in the yard. Christ. If you shift back, you'll kill her for sure. I'm coming, don't leave her.*

I won't. But please hurry.

He looked up through the eyes of his wolf when someone said his name. He had exchanged blood with Steward before so spoke to him through this link. *Come in when you get here. Please, save her. I give you whatever you need to come inside.*

She is nearly gone, Lee. I'm not sure that I can save her with just my blood. You might...we might have to think of something else. Lee didn't ask him what that something else might be, but begged him to come and help her. *I'm coming. Nearly there.*

Save her. Steward only stood in the doorway then, his body casting a dark shadow across him and Kimber. *Please, you have to save her. She's all I have. I need her.*

I cannot cross the line. Lee tried again to tell him to come in. Nothing was going to work unless Lee let go of Kimber, and they both knew that she would surely die. *Is there anyone else at home? That lives here?*

There wasn't. And he told him so. *Hannah is at school, and there isn't any live-in help. Is there anything you can do? Anything at all?* Steward said he would return. In only moments, but what seemed an eternity, not only did he return, but he had little Hannah in his arms. *Steward, what the fuck are you doing?*

Ignoring him for the moment, Steward looked at Hannah and pointed to her mother lying naked on the floor. "Hannah, your mother is hurt. See her? I need your help so that I can save her. I don't know if I can or not, but I need your help because there is no one else." Lee whimpered, his wolf never leaving Kimber's side. Twice now he knew that her heart had stopped beating completely, and both times he'd begged her to live. "I have to have you go into the house and let me in. Do you understand me? You have to give me permission to be able to cross the line to enter to help her."

"Yes. I understand you." Hannah looked at Lee before speaking again. "I trusted you not to hurt her. Now look what you did. She might die because of you."

As soon as she told Steward that he could come in, he flew across the room and tore at Kimber's throat. Lee's wolf backed away from her, but he never left, not even when Hannah tried to drag him away. After Steward tore at his wrist and put it to Kimber's throat, Hannah sat near her mom but wouldn't look at Lee. When Hunter arrived, he went to get Kimber a blanket and wrapped her in it while they all watched and waited. It wasn't long before Steward looked at him.

"It might be too late." Lee nodded at Steward. "I'm sorry. I don't know...I don't think I can save her. Not like this. She's lost a great deal of blood, and her body is weaker than I know how to heal."

Lee didn't want to leave her, but he had to shift. He needed to be with her, needed to hold her if only for the last time. When he left her, Hunter said he'd watch her, but it was Hannah that hurt him the most. Lee's wolf had moved close to her to touch her, and she smacked him in the face. The pain of it, and there was a great deal, was no more than he deserved for what he'd done to her and her mother.

"Don't come near me, you monster. You killed my mommy and I hate you. Both of you. Don't touch either of us again. I hope you die too."

Lee moved out of the room, his heart lying on the floor

dying with the woman that he loved more than anything. He heard Hannah sobbing and Hunter trying to comfort her when Steward said again that he was worried he was too late. He'd not been too late. This was not Steward's fault, but his. Lee had done this all on his own. He'd killed the only woman that he would ever love. Instead of going to their room to shift and to dress, he moved out of the house and to the wooded area behind it. There he did the only thing he could do...he ran until he fell over. Hopefully for the very last time.

Lee

CHAPTER 11

Hunter moved through the woods trying his best to find Lee. This was the fifth day in a row that they'd been searching, and he was afraid they were never going to find him. The river was high right now with the snow melting off the hill behind the house, and he didn't want to think of his brother's body being found by some fisherman in a few months. The others were looking too. Even the wild wolves were out hunting. Wherever he was, he was hidden well because he would not think any more of him being dead. But he was afraid that his brother might have done something very stupid.

Find him? He told his dad that he had not. *Well, are you looking hard enough? I swear to you, I'm going to have to come out there and find him myself, aren't I? He needs to come home and make some arrangements. I can't...I don't want to...where is my boy, Hunter? Where can he be after all this time?*

I don't know, Dad, and I'm looking. We all are. He was in a great deal of pain, and maybe he just needs a little more time. He felt his dad's pain and wanted to go to him and comfort him as well. *Is Hannah still not talking?*

Won't say a word. I even tried to get her to play a game with me. Not even little Kelly had any luck with her. Just sits there in that chair and looks out the window. Never seen a child so heart sick in my life. Not even when your own mother passed have I seen anyone so broken up. Hunter knew her pain but not how to fix it. *And I don't know when she ate last. Several days for sure. What are we going to do with them?*

It had been five days since he'd been called to the house by his brother. Five long and horribly terrible days just waiting and watching. When Steward had taken Kimber away with him, Hannah had moved to the stairs and gone to her room. She'd not been out once, so far as he knew, and he'd had someone watching her at all times. He'd called to Lee to have him come home to her, to do something, but he'd not answered him either. The search parties had been going both day and night, but nothing. And then today, one of the wild wolves had come to Sloan and led her to the bloodied mess in the woods.

I think I found something. Hunter stilled in his movements, waiting for Graham to say more. *I don't think...just give me a few minutes. I don't know what I've found just yet.*

Where are you? Graham didn't answer him, but he knew that he was busy trying to figure out what he'd found. Whatever it was, it couldn't be good. *Graham, I need to come to you. What is it you've found?*

A body. It's not Lee, but it's been torn to shit by an animal. But not Lee's wolf. I don't smell him on the man at all. He felt the air leave his body, along with about ten or so years of his life. It wasn't his brother's body, his mind kept telling him. Not Lee. *I'm putting down a marker so we can find it later. I think it's the mate to the woman that I found. I think that they've been...he's been murdered too. Christ, Hunter, who would do such a thing?*

Hunter leaned against the tree where he was standing when a falcon landed in front of him. He was startled by it, but then realized it was Dawn. She shifted but didn't move for several seconds while she stood so still. She and Ellis had arrived the first day, and she'd been out as all her animals looking in places that none of them could.

"I found him. I want to tell you that he's alive first off. But he's in a bad way." He nodded. "Before I take you to him, you should know that he has a gun. And he's not right in the head. His grief is almost something you can touch. And he's...he's pretty messed up physically as well. Not sure of the extent of his wounds, but he's hurt." He asked her if he was nearby. "Yes. He's...Hunter, please don't...I think he's going to die down there. If he does then you'll never get his body out. I think that's his plan, to die where no one can get him and he'll just rot. He doesn't think well of himself right now."

"I'm sure he doesn't, but I can't let him do that. You know that as well as I do. He has to come out, if only to be with Hannah." Dawn nodded but still didn't move. "What else is there? I have a feeling that you're trying to figure out a way to tell me."

"I am. He's...I don't think that he's going to be okay. I think...I'm sure that he's going to wish you'd never found him. I'm almost wishing that I hadn't. He is hurting." Hunter said he knew that. "No, I don't think you do. He's killed his mate. He has. And he's not just blaming himself for it, but his wolf too. I think that he might be better off simply using the gun on himself."

Hunter felt his heart ache. Not just for his brother, but for all of them. Kimber had died that day, and there had been nothing, not a thing, anyone could have done to save her. And if they lost him as well, if Lee were to die out here, even by his own hand, none of them would be the same again.

As he made his way to where she told him to go, Hunter let the others know what was going on. Dad was the most upset. He wanted to be there but couldn't leave Hannah, or wouldn't leave her. He had been the only one that she'd let near her. And the only one that could get her to go to the bathroom and then to bed. When Hunter got to the small downward cave he nearly waited on the others, but heard the wolf howl. It was the loneliest sound he'd ever heard. The echo of it seemed to call him to come down to it. To save them.

It took him nearly twenty minutes to make his way down the deep and sometimes too narrow passage. He heard his brother twice more, and each time it echoed upward to him, making him want to turn and run, leave him there as Dawn had suggested.

"Lee." He turned to him, his eyes wild with something that nearly made Hunter back up. The light from the opening above him seemed to highlight every part of him, the feral parts of him. "I need you to come with me. You have everyone worried."

"Go away." His wolf nearly snarled at him with Lee's voice. "Go away and leave me to rot."

"Hannah needs you." Lee sobbed, his body nearly bent with it. "She's suffering too. The poor thing hasn't eaten or slept much in the last five days. You need to come and see to her. If you don't, then she'll die as well. And I know that's not what you want, not for Kimber's child."

"She hates me because I killed her mother. Not that I blame her. I hate me too. Very much." Hunter knew that was true. And he was pretty sure that her hatred of Lee wasn't nearly as bad as his own was for himself. "Go away, Hunter. Just go away. I'm not...I don't want to live anymore."

"You're going to break Sloan's heart. She's hurting so badly that the baby knows it too. Neither of them are doing well." Lee continued to cry and Hunter had to sit down. "Lee, please, I can't lose you. You're my brother."

"He killed her. My wolf did. He wouldn't listen to me when I begged him to let her go. I knew once he bit into her that it wasn't going to work, but he kept at it. I don't think he meant to kill her, but she's dead all the same. What am I going to do without her, Hunter? I'm not even sure I want...I just want to die here. Please, just leave me here." Lee continued to look away as he spoke quietly. "I'm going to kill us. I know as well as you do what will happen if I don't. We'll both turn, and then you'll have to do it anyway. I can't let you live with that. This is bad enough, knowing that I hurt another, and Hannah will never forgive me anyway."

"I won't have to. Come with me and we'll think of something. Please?" Lee didn't move, and Hunter wiped at the tears that seemed to stream down his face. "Lee, you have to come out of here. You can't die here, even if I thought I could let you. I need for you to come out of here and back to the house with us."

"She was so happy, did you know that? Kimber was so happy with our house, and even the school that we got Hannah in. She was feeling pretty good about her aunt too, and the way that things were going with her. Even the thought

161

of Hannah's grandparents, while daunting, didn't bother her that much. The restaurant was going to be hers, she'd told me on her way to the house. Then she comes home and I kill her." Hunter tried to tell him that she knew that he loved her, and that was important too. "Yeah, some love of her life I turned out to be. I killed her."

"Hunter?" He turned to see who was coming toward them, and stood up when he couldn't make out the voice. "Hunter, where are you, man? I need to speak to you and Lee."

"Steward?" The man seemed to appear in front of him, and it was all he could do not to cringe from him when he smiled. When he was offered a hand to stand up, he took it, knowing that Steward would never hurt him. "What the hell are you...? I thought you had gone to ground. That's what you said when I tried to reach you the other day."

"I did. We did." He smiled bigger. "Damn, that was the most difficult thing I've ever done. But it worked. My home soil is the only thing that I could think of when what I was doing for her just wasn't working. It was all I could do to get us there and bury us as deeply as I could in it. She's not happy with me, to say the least, but it worked."

"What the hell are you talking about?" They both looked at Lee when he sobbed again. "I have to get him out of here. Do you think you can pick him up and transport him out for me? But be careful. He has a gun." Steward turned back to the way he'd come, and Hunter looked as well. If there was someone else to help out, Hunter thought for sure they were going to need it. "Who's there?"

"Kimber." Steward looked at him when he asked him what he said. "Kimber. She's not very good at this lifestyle just yet. I'm not sure, to be honest with you, how much of her is vampire or wolf. But I had her do a few things, tests really, to understand what she might be able to do. All of them, with the exception of a couple of things, she did without any trouble."

"Steward. This isn't funny. Not even for you." Then he saw her. Kimber moved out of the shadows and into the small light that just barely reached her. She looked...well, different was an understatement. And when she was within touching distance of him, he knew what it was. "She's a vampire."

"That's what I was trying to tell you. She has some of the traits, but not all. Sun doesn't seem to bother her, we discovered. And she can eat food. But the rest...." Steward shrugged. "I don't have any idea what she can or can't do for now, but she's alive. And she's healed as well. Additionally, she's immortal. Just as I am."

"Kimber?" Lee stood up and moved toward her. Hunter had a moment of panic when she backed away from him. Not that he blamed her...Lee looked horrific. "Kimber? It is really you? I've seen you so much over the last several days. Is it you?"

His brother's face looked gaunt and half starved. There were cuts on his mouth, cheeks, and forehead. And not having anything to eat or drink had taken its toll on him in that his skin was dry and cracked. He was cut and bleeding all over his body, and it looked as if he'd broken his arm. Hunter wondered if he had tried to shift through it, but knew that he'd not. He was pissed at his wolf for what he thought he'd done. Steward pulled him back when Kimber moved toward Lee.

Steward told him it was time they left them there. "What if she can't bring him out? What if they both simply die down here?"

"She won't die and neither will he. Also, she's been to see Hannah. Not for long, but long enough that the little girl knows that her mommy is alive." Steward led the way out of the cave. "I don't know if the rift between Lee and Hannah will heal quite as quickly, but Kimber told her that she loves him and needs him in her life."

"Hannah hates him. I think she blames him for all of this. While that's true to a point, his wolf needed her as a part of him." Steward nodded. "I tried talking to Hannah, but she won't speak to any of us. I'm glad…Christ, Steward, this has been one hell of a few days. I can't…I can't thank you enough for what you've done for my family. We were all…we all thought she was dead. None of us…it's been hard. So thank you very much." Hunter gave a tiny but stressed laugh before speaking again. "Do you think you could have at least told us you had her and she was alive? We've been grieving like she was dead."

Steward laughed and Hunter hugged him. Then when emotions overwhelmed him again, he hugged him tighter. Hunter couldn't begin to think how to repay the man. He owed him anything and everything that he'd ever ask for.

"She was dead, Hunter. When I left you, her heart was no longer beating and there was no blood flow to her brain or any other part of her. I took her to my home to try…I was going to bury her so that you'd not have to, but when I got her there she…she touched me. Not physically, but mentally. Hunter, she's going to surprise you with her strength now. And I don't mean just her physical strength. She's a telepath as well as a few other things. Things that I gave her."

Hunter didn't care and told him that. "She's alive, and if she can bring Lee around, then I don't care if she can take me on and win as alpha. I can't lose him. And thanks to you, I won't lose any of them." Steward nodded and said nothing else as they made their way out into the waning light. He looked at his family, all of them standing there, and wondered how they'd made it so quickly. Then he looked at Sloan holding their daughter and went to her. Nothing else mattered right now but all of them. He needed to be with his mate now, and his brother was going to be just fine.

~~~

"Is it really you?" Kimber nodded, not really sure what to say to him. Everything seemed to be so much right now, it was all she could do not to leap away and try to shut some of it out. Even his scent, strong and dirty smelling, made her slightly ill. "I thought you were dead."

"I was. I guess. For a while there, I think even Steward thought so." She let him touch her and felt something inside of her curl up against her skin. "I like that. But you stink."

"I guess I do." He was naked too. His cock seemed to grow along with his touching her face. "I should go back to the house and take a bath."

"You should." She wrapped her arms around him and smiled. It was one of the first things that Steward had shown her how to use. "I'm not really very good at this, so I want you to hold onto me. Don't let me go, okay?"

He said that he would hold on, and she felt his cock thicken at her pussy. Closing her eyes, trying her best not to think about how much she needed him, Kimber tried to remember everything in their room, where things were placed and where she could land them. When she opened her eyes, she smiled. She'd done it. And she'd not landed in anything this time. Lee tried to guide her to the bed as he kissed and nibbled at her throat.

"No. You need to bathe. I'm not kidding when I tell you that you really stink." He laughed, then looked around the room they were in. She watched his face turn from joyful to something akin to fear. "Lee, I'm not the same person I was before. I'm...he said that he'd either change me or bury me. I don't know about you, but I'm kind of glad to be here. With you and Hannah. Are you?"

"Yes. I'm very glad you're here with us. I think...I had no idea that he had done...I'm fine now that you're not dead." His finger grazed over her skin, and that movement was there again. "I can feel her. Your wolf. I guess it worked."

"Come on. I need to get you into the shower. I need to make sure that you're not too hurt. Can you shift? I think your arm is broken." He backed away from her like she'd hit him. "Lee? What is it? Are you afraid of me? Please don't be."

"I'm not. I know...I'm not going to shift. Not ever if I can help it. Especially while you're in the room with me." She moved toward him to touch him. "How can you even want me to after what he...what we did to you? We nearly killed you. I won't put you in that position again. Not ever."

"But you didn't kill me, Lee. I'm still here." Kimber moved toward him slowly, and he looked terrified. "I'm just fine now. A little more than I was before. But I'm here now. You're hurt, you need to fix it. Please, just let your wolf help you so you can be all right."

"No."

She wasn't sure what to do and reached for Steward. But he told her that she could contact Hunter and should ask him. He told her that while he was friends with wolves, he had no more idea what to do than she did. As Lee moved to the bathroom, it felt like he closed more than just the door; he closed off a part of her heart too.

If you don't get him to shift, I can command him to. It will be extremely painful for him and might hurt him more than if he just healed his arm on his own. And that's not a guarantee that he'll want to shift again. He needs you to prove to him that he's not going to hurt you. She felt his embarrassment and then the laughter. *Get him...I can't believe I'm telling you this, but get him aroused. Then you shift. It might pull his own wolf should you do that.*

And if it doesn't? Hunter said he would do it for her. *I'll get him to do this. I'm not sure how...aroused, huh? Okay then. Will you keep an eye on Hannah for me? I'm not sure how long this will take. I'm not exactly a femme fatale.*

Take as long as you need. We'll have her at our house. Dad has decided that the three of them, including Kelly, need to do some fishing in the morning. Drowning worms is more like it, but they have fun. He wants to get them to help him gather their gear. I have no idea what he thinks he can do in the middle of the night, but that's my dad. Hannah had talked of nothing else but fishing with her grandda before this happened. *Kimber, you're going to do just fine, and I can't tell you enough how happy I am that you're still a part of our family.*

Kimber thanked him and moved to the bathroom door. She could hear the water running, almost hear each drop of it going down the drain. Getting used to being able to hear everything had nearly made her mad the first day—was that only yesterday? But now she had learned to think of a volume control knob and turning it down. Opening the door, she moved into the room and started to strip down.

Kimber had no more idea how to seduce a man than she did how to rebuild an engine on a car. But as she took off her clothing, she thought of what she loved about Lee when he made love to her. She went to the shower and let out a long breath. Opening the large door, she moved up behind him and wrapped her arms around him.

"You should have waited for me to be finished. I'm almost done." He wasn't, but she kissed his muddy skin anyway. Reaching above his head, Kimber pulled the bottle of soap and the large sponge off and filled it. "Kimber, please, just let me do this on my own. I just need a few minutes, then I'll be done here and you can take one."

He was nervous, she realized then. At what she had no idea, but his arm cradled against his body made her ache to help him. And if this worked she was going to give Hunter a nice gift. Not having a clue what to get a man that had it all, she knew that she'd have to make it special. She thought of giving her daughter a bath when she was little, then the soaps that had meant so much to her.

"When Hannah and I were in France, there was this little shop about a block from our house. They sold the most amazing soaps and candles. I couldn't afford them, of course, but I did love to go in and just smell them. There was one that smelled like the earth. Like you do. Not dirty, but earthy I guess." Rubbing the soapy sponge down his back, she was happy when he didn't tell her to go away again. "One year Fern got me a bottle of this strawberry soap for my birthday. I used it only when I needed a pick-me-up. Which, now that I think about it, was almost every day. I might see if they have a shop online and see about getting some."

Washing the mud from his back, she saw all the cuts that he'd gotten. Kissing the first one she saw, Kimber ran her tongue over it and was surprised to see it heal almost immediately. Doing the same for the rest of them, she heard his heart rate pick up, and went to her knees to wash his legs.

The water coming off him wasn't nearly as dark now. The soap bubbles made pretty swirls as they went down the drain. Washing his legs, she wasn't surprised to see that he'd cut himself there as well, and licked the one on his inner thigh. His moan had her running her tongue over it twice more before she moved to his feet.

"You're not going to change my mind about this." She asked him about what. "Shifting. I'm not going to do it when you're around. I don't want to hurt you again. I know that as a vampire you're sort of a super person, but I won't hurt you again."

"You're not going to." This time she ran her fangs down his leg, and then nipped at him until she drew blood. Licking the fresh taste of him, Kimber moaned and then licked him again. "You taste different now. Your blood is spicy and hotter. Is it because I can taste it better, or is it because you're so aroused?"

Turning him was work. He fought her as much as he could, but she won in the end. His cock was so hard and stretched from him that she leaned into him and licked the thick cream at the tip. He curled his hands into her hair and held her there before pulling her back.

"I feel him. Your wolf." Rubbing her head against his thigh, Kimber moaned when he did. "I can smell him too. He wants to taste me, doesn't he?"

Lee's voice was strangled, his "No" nearly hard to understand. But when she took him into her mouth, his crown and as much of his shaft as she could, he rocked into her over and over until she felt his wolf again. Cupping his balls in her hand, she sucked him hard, feeling his balls tighten against his body even as she held him. When he pulled from her, she knew that he was going to tell her to back off, but he jerked her from the floor and lifted her.

"I need to fuck you like this. Christ, I need you." His cock slammed into her as he pressed her against the wall of the shower. His mouth moved from hers to her throat, where she felt his teeth graze her skin. He never bit her, but he did growl low. Kimber moved his head to the side and licked the pounding pulse, then sank her fangs deep into his throat.

The taste was amazing. Overwhelming and somehow not enough. As she swallowed, her mouth filled again and she heard him cry out, his body pounding her harder than he had before as he emptied inside of her. Kimber loved it. Sealing the wound at his throat, she pulled his head up and looked into his eyes.

"Bite me." He tried to shake her off. "Bite me now, Lee. Taste me."

He growled again, and she felt her pussy tighten. When her head was jerked to the right, he didn't bother with licking the flesh so that the pain would be lessened, but bit her deeply, tearing at her skin as she screamed out her first release. Lee lifted his head then, his mouth covered in her blood, his wolf, so close to the surface, seeming to beg her for something. Doing the only thing she could think of, she pulled from him and let the wolf take her.

Lee turned the water off and stared at her. She knew that she was making his wolf wild with need. Not only could she feel him, but her wolf could as well and wanted him to come out and play. So when she licked his thigh, then his cock, she backed from him and nearly fell on the tile floor. Moving into the room, pacing back and forth, Kimber reached deep inside of Lee and called for his wolf.

Come to me. The wolf snarled at her, and she could see the affect it was having on Lee. He was fighting her, fighting both of them. But she had a feeling that the two of them were winning. Kimber called to him again.

The wolf took him. Not easily either, if his cries were any indication. She watched as he shook his huge body, then looked at her with his teeth showing and his fur standing on end. But for some reason, even with all his anger, she wasn't afraid of him. Instead she moved to him and rubbed her body to his.

You don't play fair. Kimber laughed. *But I will say this for you, you are the most beautiful wolf I've ever seen. Christ, you're red. Do you know how rare that is?*

No. I only know that she makes me feel like I can take on the world. Especially with you at my side.

Moving along his skin again, she went to the door. Turning to look at him, she flicked her tail at him and moved out. She knew that he'd follow her.

The stairs were harder to maneuver than she would have thought. But once she was down them, the hardwood floor of the hallway was a little slippery. She did manage to fall a couple of times before she realized there had to be a trick to this. Kimber heard Lee laughing at her as she tried to get her feet under her, and turned to look at him.

It's all in the way you step. Walk like you would as a human on ice. Just keep your feet under you and take smaller steps. He laughed again when all four of her feet went out from under her and she fell on her body. *You're still thinking of yourself as two footed. You need to walk on all four at the same time.*

Well, come here and show me, smart ass. When he made it to the door without falling, she could have stomped her foot. And she might have had she not been afraid of falling again. The door, thankfully, had been left slightly ajar or they might not have gotten outside. As soon as she felt the earth under her feet, Kimber knew a new kind of joy.

CHAPTER 12

Lee watched her running around like a small child, leaping in mid-air, then landing on her feet. He sat back and laughed at her antics until she fell once and didn't get up. But as he approached her, he saw why she was so still. The deer had come out to eat.

They're beautiful. He told her that they'd been around since he'd bought the house. *We'll have to make sure that we feed them this winter too. I don't want them to come to harm.*

They won't here. He moved up beside her, careful to not frighten the little herd. *Last spring that little guy with the buttons on his head was just a baby. This year I bet we have a few more.*

I can smell them. And while they smell like meat to me, I can smell something else about *them too. What is that?* He lifted his head to the air and let the scents come to him. He could smell it then and lay down beside Kimber as the deer ate by moonlight.

Two of them are breeding. I think the darker one with the light spot on her nose and the one that is closest to the buck. It's hard to tell from here, but I think maybe this fall. We'll have to make sure they have more than enough food for the offspring too. Lee laid his head on her and thought about her being gone from him.

I'm all right. He nipped at her shoulder but said nothing. *I was terrified when I woke up. I was…the dirt was so dark and there wasn't anyone close to me. Then I felt Steward. He wasn't breathing, and I thought we'd been buried alive and that he'd not survived. He told me that when he needs to, like when he's really hurt, he can go there and feel better in hours. I guess that's why he took me there.*

He told us…when you were bleeding out that he wasn't going to be able to save you. She said nothing as he continued. *I left without making sure. I could have been there for you when you woke. But…well, Hannah was hurting too and I know that it's no excuse, but I couldn't help me, much less her.*

I don't think that would have been a good thing had you been there when I woke. I wasn't really…I wasn't right in the head. And I might have hurt you. I know that I did Steward. Lee told her good. *He was really kind and gentle with me. Told me over and over that you were all right and that Hannah was as well. I guess…he said that I'd have some of him and you in my body forever.*

Yes. I'm guessing that while my wolf changed you, it was too much on your body. You've been under a lot of pressure and stress lately, and you weren't up to your full strength. I don't know what I would have done had…well, I know what I did. I was going to kill myself. A wolf without his mate goes rogue, wild, and kills for no reason other than it is in their nature. My dad was lucky that he had us when Mom died, but there were times that it was close. I was nearly there as well. He watched the deer as he thought of Hannah. *She doesn't trust me, she said. I hurt her too when…*

Steward had to go and get her from her school to have her invite him into the house. She hates me.

She was scared, but she doesn't hate you. I think...the two of you will be fine. I know that. I talked to her before coming to find you. And your dad. He's going to come and stay with us for a little while. Then he said he wants to find his own home. I think he's sweet on Mabel. Lee told her he thought she was right. *I have to talk to Hannah about this. About what happened. She might be a little cool toward you for a little while, but I think she'll come around quickly.*

He hoped so. Lee loved the little girl so very much. When the deer were startled out of their dinner, he stood up as well. There were things that he wanted to show her on their property, and now was as good a time as ever. Plus, he wanted to take her to the boundaries of his land and that of the neighbor. A man that wasn't all that nice.

I'd like to have a baby with you. Lee nearly fell over the log he was stepping over. *Soon. I want several, but I want us to have this one now.*

You're not in heat. He felt his inner self flush at his words. *That came out wrong. Wolves have to be in heat to have a baby. It happens several times a year. We can try when you...why are you shaking your head like that?*

I'm not all wolf. I'm vampire too. He nodded, not sure what she meant. *I can have one whenever you want. Whenever we want. I asked Steward about it when we were talking about my new and awesome powers.*

Awesome powers, huh? And just what kind of powers do you have? He sat down, his wolf as amused as he was. But when she shifted, her body coming out of the wolf dressed and beautiful, he whimpered. *You can do that? Christ, you're beautiful in either form.*

"You will be able to as well when you drink from me again, this time deeply." The wolf seemed to like that idea and moved toward her. But Lee was terrified of biting her again. He could still see her when she'd been as white as a ghost with blood all around her. "You'll have to sooner or later, Lee. I need you to be like me."

Like you how? We're already wolf, so what else is there? She moved toward him, her body seeming to shimmer in the moonlight. *Stay back, please. He wants you.*

"And I want him. He likes to lick me until I come, doesn't he? Drink from my wet pussy over and over until I can't move. Then he marks me, and that makes me spin with pleasure. Do you know how hard I come when he does that?" He told her to stay back again, but she began to undress. There wasn't much to remove, a shift of a dress and then her panties. "Come here and show me how much you enjoy my body, Lee. Come and taste me until I come down his throat, then fuck me as a man."

No. But his wolf, like before, was winning out. Not that Lee wasn't enjoying her this way, but he wasn't going to bite her. *Kimber, I don't want to hurt you again. I can't do that to you, ever.*

"I'm an immortal, Lee. If you bite me now, all you're going to do is drink my blood. And then I want to bite you." He felt his wolf shimmer along his body in agreement with her plan. "You only need to drink from me once to get what I have to offer. Then twice more and you'll be just like me. A vampire that can be wolf too. I want to feel you inside of me, Lee. Please come here and eat me."

His wolf lunged at her when she sat on the ground. Her body was open for him, and when his wolf licked her from gate to clit, he threw back his head and howled. Kimber cried out with her release. Then she looked at him.

"Bite me." The wolf moved slower this time. He whimpered slightly again before licking the long length of her thigh. When he nudged her thigh up, Kimber lifted her leg and his wolf sank his teeth into her gently but firmly. This time Kimber cried out with the powerful release. As soon as he licked the wound closed, Lee knew the difference in her taste but didn't think on it too much.

His wolf wanted more. He wanted it all. As he ate at her, using his tongue to bring her several more times, Lee thought of her taste, and how her blood had felt filling his body. And it had too, filled his cells until he felt like he was all powerful. When he lifted his head up, Lee took his body back and watched Kimber as she sat up and smiled at him.

Burying his mouth over her heat, he slid his fingers into her and curled them around until she flooded him with her cream. Every time he touched her, set off tremors in her that he'd never been able to touch before, she cried out his name over and over until she was hoarse from it. Lifting his body up, Lee made his way up hers until he paused at her breast. Even they felt different, tasted better as well.

"Fuck me." He nodded at her command but didn't move to fill her. He wanted to take his time with her. Fill her slowly and make her come around him while he watched. "Please. You've teased me enough."

"You've come more times than I've ever imagined. Who is teasing who?" He suckled at her breast again and then bit down on the pert nipple. Tasting blood, he licked the tiny wound closed. Fisting his cock, he teased her clit as he felt her heat pull at him.

"Please? Please, I need you." He told her he needed her as

well. "Fill me, Lee. Please stop this before I hurt you."

He entered her slowly, his body aching to fill her completely. Lee moved in and out of her, filling her then taking away until he was buried to the root. Lying atop her, all he could think about was how he felt at home, his heart and soul belonged to no one but her. As she wrapped her legs around him he moved carefully, trying his best to make it last. As sweat slid down his back, his cock aching to fill her again, Lee leaned to her throat and felt his teeth shift in his mouth. As he bit down, tearing once more into her flesh, he felt as if he fell in love with her all over again. Filling her with his seed, Lee hoped that they made a child so that the world would know how much he loved his mate. When she cried out her own pinnacle, Lee knew that for as long as he lived no one could touch his heart the way that she did at this very moment.

He lay there atop her, trying his best to catch his breath when she touched her fingers to his back. Lifting his head, Lee looked down at her and she smiled at him. Lee kissed her then, taking from her as much as she was giving him.

"I love you." He grinned at her. "Well, I do. I have never said that to anyone before. Not even Hannah's father. I thought I loved him, but I know better now. This is everything. I know the difference now between what we had and what you and I have."

"And I love you. Very much." She looked so sad that he held her to him as he rolled them to his back. "I'm so sorry that I hurt you. I never meant for that to happen."

"I know that. Even when I knew that I was dying, I knew it. You're a wonderful man, and I could not have asked for a more loving and kind person in our lives right now." Lee thought about Hannah and hurt for what he'd done to her.

"I'll talk to her, I promise. I'm not sure of what all happened, but she'll come around. It just might take her a few days."

"I'm going to work on this too. I have a few things in mind to win her over." Kimber asked him what. "You just let me handle it. If I fuck up, you can step in, but this is between the two of us now. All right?"

"Yes." He could hear that she was a little leery of what he had planned, but he knew this would work. Lee was willing to get down on his hands and knees for her if that was what it took. "You love her, don't you?"

"Yes. As much as I do you." He added another thing to his list of things that he wanted to do for Hannah, but knew that he'd need Kimber's permission for that. "I want to adopt her. Give her my name. Not right now, but soon. I want her to be my daughter in all ways."

"I think she'd like that very much. And if that is what she wants, then I'm all for it." He nodded when she sat up. Lee watched her as she closed her eyes. Then just like that, she was dressed. "Steward said that you might be able to do this too if you think on it hard enough. But he did say that you're about as stubborn as Sloan is rich."

He started to deny it but didn't. Instead, he tried to think of ways to get back at his friend. As he stood up, he also wondered if this thing with dressing would work too. But almost as soon as he thought of it, he was standing with a suit and tie on, his usual mode of dress.

"Yeah, that's got to go." He thought of jeans and a tee-shirt as she laughed at him. "Better, but you do know that it's the middle of May? I'm thinking shorts and no shirt."

"It's also the middle of May in Ohio. We won't be ready for shorts until June or July. It can be seventy today and ten below tomorrow." They were both laughing when they got back to the house. The sun was just coming up over the horizon. Lee didn't think he could have been any happier.

~~~

Kimber watched Hannah. She was completely ignoring every attempt Lee was making to bring her over to his side. Not that she wasn't caving a little, but Hannah was strong willed, something that Kimber had just begun to notice about her daughter.

"I'm sorry. Sorrier than I could ever be about what you saw. Steward is too, as a matter of fact." Still nothing from her, and Kimber could see that Lee was getting frustrated. "Steward had to go and get you, or you would never have had to see your mom that way."

"I wouldn't have had to see her like that either if you hadn't tried to kill her." Lee looked as if he'd been slapped. Before Kimber could say anything to him or her daughter, Hannah continued. "You tore her up and left her for dead. You couldn't even stay and make sure she was all right. You always make sure someone is okay before you run away. Why should I trust you anymore?"

"I didn't want to live." Hannah looked at Lee when he spoke softly. "I wanted to die after I did that to her. And when you told me that you would never like me again or trust me, my heart just fell silent. There wasn't anything I had left to live for. Not when the two people that I love more than I do my own life were no longer going to be a part of it."

"You hurt me." Lee nodded and put his hand over Hannah's. This time she didn't jerk away from him. "When Steward came and got me he looked so scared. And then I had to be there while my momma lay there dying."

"I know. I was wrong. I'd like to blame it on my wolf, but I won't. He's as much a part of me as I am him. We both love your mother and you." Hannah moved her hand but didn't take it from his. When she wiped at her tears with her free hand, Kimber wanted to snatch her up into her arms and protect her. "I love you, Hannah. With all my heart, and I hope that someday you'll forgive me for what I did to you and your mom."

Lee got up and kissed Hannah on the head, then walked out of the house. Neither of them said a word as Lee's truck started up and then left the drive. Kimber got up to start working on dinner, as Sloan and Hunter were coming over with the baby later to go over some of the specs on the new restaurant. Kimber also had a contract from Luke that Shawn had given her from Clemmie about the new art building. But her mind was more on the little girl at the table than any of that.

"Is he coming back?" Kimber asked her who. "Lee. Is he coming back to live here with us or is he running away again?" She didn't care for her tone but said nothing about it for now.

"He's got a job to do, like I have one. I think today he's having a meeting with the school board where you go. Something about lunch programs and what they serve." Hannah got up and came to stand by her at the big butcher block table where she was working. "He thinks you're right in what they serve, and he wanted to look into it."

"Why? It won't make me like him." Kimber just looked at Hannah. "I'm sorry. That was really mean. I didn't...I did mean it, but it was still mean."

"It was. He's not doing this for you. As you said to us last week, there are some kids that don't have someone at home to cook breakfast for them, and he's offering his services and money. Some already go to the diner where I work in the early morning, but it's hard on poor Mabel to feed that many alone." Hannah watched her cut up the salmon into four inch square filets. "There are a lot of people around here that are worse off than you and I were in France. You know that."

Without saying a word, Hannah picked up the lemons that were in a big bowl and started rolling them under her hand. It would make the juices easier to use, as well as soften the pulp inside. As she reached for one of the smaller knives, Kimber watched as she carefully cut thin slices of the fruit. She didn't normally like her using the sharp knives, but she knew her daughter loved to help in the kitchen.

"I could help out."

Kimber said nothing as she put the salmon in the brine she'd prepared of soy sauce and brown sugar. She asked Hannah what she thought she could do to help. Hannah put the lemon slices in the water that had been set aside to use on the cedar planks.

When she didn't answer right away, Kimber got out the large bag of fresh asparagus that she'd bought this morning. When she'd been in the yard yesterday, talking to the gardener, he said that he knew how to grow it and told her that he could plant her some if she wanted. They had worked for over three hours on the herbs she wanted to put into a garden to use in the house. Things were coming along nicely, and she had already talked to Lee about putting in a drying shed for them.

"I know how to make french toast. And waffles. Fern let me make them when her back hurt too much." Kimber told her those were good things to know how to cook. "And I know how to make sausage links too without burning them. I can't cook like you can, but I want to help."

"I won't be helping him, but I'm sure he could use the help. I have to go and take care of the diner until they hire someone else to take over. I guess Mabel has been looking for candidates for the last couple of days. If you want to help, you'll be working with Lee." Hannah just nodded. "I have to make a salad for tonight. I know that Hunter and Sloan aren't into green things much, so what do you think we should have?"

"How about an antipasto salad? I love the olives in them." Kimber went to the refrigerator to see what they had, and started pulling things out and handing them to Hannah. "I can help Lee. It's a good project, and if he wants me to, I can be in charge of the eggs."

"You'll have to ask him about it. Like I said, that's his project. Well, both your projects, but he didn't think you'd want to work with him, so he didn't ask."

Instead of making a salad, they ended up putting together kabobs. First they put on the tortellini that had been left over from last night. It was cold now, so it slid over the sticks nicely. Next they put on chunks of salami, then cheese, cherry tomatoes, and finally Kalamata olives. After repeating this several times until the sticks were full, they laid them out on a platter and put olive oil-based dressing on them. After covering them, Hannah took them to the refrigerator in the pantry to make room for the rest of the food.

"Do you think that he'd be okay with me working with him?" Kimber nearly smiled but said that she should ask him. "He might say no."

"He might, but then you'll never know unless you ask." As Kimber went about making up the rice pilaf for dinner, making sure to only make enough for her and Hannah, she fried up some bacon bits to go with the huge baked potatoes that she'd gotten as well. "His number is in my cell phone if you want to call and ask him. When he goes to this meeting, it will be good for him to know that he has help."

Hannah nodded but didn't pick up the phone. Kimber tried her best to not beg her to do it or even to make her call him. Lee had told her that this was his project to work on Hannah, and he would be upset with her if she intruded. After the potatoes were scrubbed and rolled in bacon grease and sea salt, Hannah asked to be excused. Kimber reached for Lee as soon as her daughter left the room.

I didn't want you to think it was me and say something...well, like you did last night. His laughter made her warm all over. *We should get her a phone so that it never happens.*

Kimber had called Lee to tell him that she was headed to the grocery store. But when he'd answered it, instead of letting her talk, he started telling her what he was going to do to her when he got home, none of it appropriate for a child.

I agree on the phone. Wait, it's ringing now. I don't want to seem too excited, so let me get back to you.

Kimber made the crust for a cherry pie and set it aside. When Hannah came back in the room, she not only had the filling cooling but she'd made tea as well. Hannah just sat at the table and stared. Kimber was suddenly very worried. Then Hannah spoke.

"He said that he'd be honored to have me on his team. Honored. Not like it, but he said honored." Kimber said nothing, too overwhelmed at the moment to do much more than nod. "And he said that he was going to tell them it was my idea, something that I had come up with, and he thought that the school board should listen to me more. Why would he do that?"

"I think perhaps he values your opinion." Kimber sat down. "He really does love you, Hannah. More than anything, he is sorry for what he put you through. But he didn't do this to make you forgive him or even to love him. He talked this over with Sloan, and she is even glad that you suggested it."

The rest of dinner prep was a blur. Hannah would sit for long periods of time, then ask a question out of the blue. Kimber went from being proud of her daughter to wanting to strangle her all in a heartbeat. She thought that was the way it would always be, and tried not to let it bother her overly much. Hannah being a teenager was going to be hell, she thought.

At five o'clock, Lee returned. He had two dozen roses, one for her and one for Hannah, and a large contract with the city to make the Emerson School Lunch Project a done deal. But before Hannah could leave them in the kitchen, Lee knelt down on one knee in front of Hannah and held out a beautiful sapphire.

"I wanted to do this a while ago. I've had this in my pocket since I gave your mom hers." He looked at Kimber, then at Hannah again. "I would be the happiest man on earth if you were to be my daughter. Not just because I have married your mom, which will be soon, but for you to have my last name so that the Emerson Project can truly be yours."

"You don't have to do this." He nodded and told her he knew that. "Then why are you? I mean, if you marry my mom or not doesn't mean that much to me. It does, but she will do it even if I did really hate you."

"Do you? Hate me, I mean? Because this will never work if you do. I love you both so much that I can hardly breathe sometimes worrying about you. And it does matter to me and to your mom if you want us to be married. I won't do anything that would ever come between the two of you. Not for anything." Hannah wiped at tears again. "Ah, honey, don't cry. I can't stand to make you cry anymore."

"I love you." Kimber thought that her heart would burst when Hannah launched herself at Lee. "I love you so much, Lee. And I'm sorry I was a brat and all."

Lee held her. Kimber watched the two of them just sitting on the floor telling each other that they were sorry. Kimber could not have asked for a better man to be in her child's life than the one that was there now.

"I guess this means I can take back the pony." Hannah looked at him, then at her. "I have one in the paddock if you want to go see her. I have to be careful around her, of course. She's not too keen on me—" Hannah was out the door before he could finish. Lee looked at her. "I guess we'll be paying for riding lessons now, right?"

"Yes. And if you buy her another animal without consulting me, I will hug you until you can't breathe." Lee got up and nuzzled her neck. "I love you, Lee Emerson."

"And I love you, Kimber Emerson."

CHAPTER 13

The courtroom was filled to overflowing. Lee watched the crowd trying to move more people into the room as he held Hannah on his lap. Kimber was sitting to his right, and Hunter was on the other side of him. Sloan had opted to stay home with the baby as crowds, and this one was proving to be much larger than they thought, still bothered her. When the bailiff stood up and announced the judge, everyone quieted.

"You having a sale there, Hunter? Never had this many people in my courtroom in over fifty years of being on the bench." Everyone laughed, and then Judge Wilson pinned his eyes on Kimberly Schroeder. "I was just informed that you refused counsel. Is that true, Miss Schroeder?"

"I don't even know why I'm here, much less needing to spend my money on someone to come here and tell you that my grandniece is a terrible person." Judge Wilson asked her again if she refused anyone to sit with her. "Yes, yes. I refuse.

How much longer am I going to be here? I have things to do. And my house to get into order. I'm sure that the servants have been slacking off since you people took me away."

"You do know why you're here, don't you? I mean, you know that Kimber Emerson is suing you for the rights of her mother's will."

Kimberly huffed, and Judge Wilson asked her what she meant.

"Her mother was a fool, and this child, this ungrateful child, is worse than she was. It's mine, all of it, as it should have been from the beginning. What you need to do is tell her to follow my commands and forget this foolishness of thinking that she's going to marry someone that I don't approve of." Judge Wilson looked in their direction, then back at Kimberly. "My way is law, and the sooner you people understand that, the better things will be for everyone."

"I'm afraid you have that wrong, Miss Schroeder. I'm the law around here, and what I say goes. Now, I want to make sure you understand what is going on here. Your grandniece has filed a claim against you in accordance with her mother's will. This has nothing to do with your involvement in the death of James Walden. The state has agreed to charge you in a separate court with that."

"I don't know why that is even in question. He didn't do as I told him to, and he had to go. What would you have done if you told this man to go in and bring Kimber to you, and instead he professes that he has fallen in love with her? Not to mention, he filled her belly with a bastard child." Lee nearly stood up and hit the woman, but the judge told her to watch her language. "She is. What do you expect me to call her if not what she is?"

"I think you've said more than enough." He looked in their direction at Luke. "You wish to say something before this begins?"

"Yes, Your Honor." Luke stood up. "It is the desire of my client to have Miss Schroeder put into a facility that would care for someone of her needs. She is willing to pay for this on the condition that Miss Schroeder has no further contact with my client or any of her family, both blood and in-laws. This is not a decision that she's come to—"

"What do you mean, put me in a facility? You most certainly will not." Kimberly stood up and leaned across the table to glare at them when she cut Luke off. "Kimber, I will not tolerate you acting this way. When I get you home, there will be penance for what you've done. And don't think that brat will be coming with you either. You belong to me."

The gavel came down hard just as Kimber was standing up. Lee stood with her but said nothing as she made her way to her aunt. Hannah held his hand as tightly as he'd ever felt. The judge stopped the police, in unusual full gear, from interceding. For now.

"Why do you hate me so much? I mean, you have to if you think I'm going to just let you take my daughter from me, let you continue to ruin my life, and let you dictate what I do or don't do. I'm a grown woman with a mind of my own." Kimberly huffed at her. "You, however, are a mean, evil woman who has gone her whole life bullying people into doing what you want, and if that didn't work, you had them killed."

"So? What would you have me do? Let you decide what is right for yourself? You've done so well on that all by yourself, haven't you? Look at you. You're a failure; and not only that, but stupid as well. If I hadn't stepped in when I did, your mother would have simply spent the money as if she didn't have a care in the world. Well, I showed her too, didn't I?" Kimber asked her how she'd done that. "It will amaze you what a few dollars here or there can get you. A terminal cancer diagnosis. Even a suicide marking on a death certificate should you need it to appear so. Your mother was a fool to think that she could do what you're trying to do. I will not be put away like some sort of animal."

"My mother didn't have cancer?" Kimberly laughed and shook her head at Kimber's question. "I was wrong about you. You're not evil, you're nuts."

The slap was loud, but before he could go to Kimber and protect her from another blow, Cash was there. His gun was out and pointed at Kimberly's head even before any of the police could get theirs cleared of their holsters. Lee was as shocked by the fact that his dad had a gun as he was that he'd gotten it into the courtroom today. Kimberly screamed to be released, and Cash looked at Lee and told him to get Kimber and Hannah out of there.

Lee made his way to the front of the courtroom to where Kimber was standing, staring at the woman who had hurt her so much. He didn't want anyone else to be hurt. The police had finally gotten their guns out and were now pointing them at anyone or anything that moved. When he put Hannah on the floor to reach for Kimber to bring her to him, Hannah moved to her aunt.

"I hate you." The woman spat at her. "You're just mean and evil like my momma said you are. And now my new grandda is going to have to shoot you dead so that you'll leave us alone."

"Get away from me, you spawn of the devil. I care not what you think of me, but your mother will when I'm finished with her." Hannah looked up at Lee as Kimberly continued with her threats. "Let me go this minute. I demand that you listen to me and tell that…that thing to go back to where she came from. Let me go or I'll have your badge. Do you hear me?"

"I hear you. Everyone hears you. You're loud enough that the entire town can hear what sort of bullshit you're spewing." Cash winked at Hannah. "You go on with your dad and mom now, honey. We got this."

Hannah turned to Lee. "Do you want to be my dad? I've been thinking about it, and I want to be your little girl with your name like you said. The sooner the better, I'm thinking."

"All right." Lee felt stupid and knelt down to her. "How about we go and get some lunch? If Grandda has this, then we can bet he'll make sure that we're all right. Whatcha think there, daughter of mine?"

As they started to leave the courtroom through the double set of doors that had been closed when the judge came to the dais, Judge Wilson was yelling for order. Luke stopped Lee as they were leaving. He asked to speak to Kimber alone, and Lee sat down with Hannah when Luke led her down the hall to an open doorway. When Hannah leaned against him on the bench, Lee knew that things were going to be just fine from now on.

~~~

"What do you want to do?" Kimber asked him what he meant. "Well, she's going away for a long time now. Not only has she assaulted a few of the officers in there, but Dad found a gun on her. Not to mention she told the entire room that she basically killed your mother and had documents falsified in her favor."

"She murdered her, didn't she? I mean, we already figured that out, but to hear her say it without any kind of remorse is just so…she really is off her head, isn't she?" Luke nodded sadly. "But I don't know what you mean. What can I do?"

"There are many options. One is that you have her committed, as was your plan. Then you'd care for her, via a third party, until she is gone. Or you let the state take care of her. Which I will say won't be as nice as what you could provide. And the third option, the one that I would do if I were you, is to let her go to trial. It won't be long in coming. The judge will try to get it worked in quickly to have her off the streets. And while she's away, which I'm thinking will be in a nice state-run facility, you can get on with your life." Kimber asked him what he thought she'd get if she went to trial. "A prison sentence that she won't outlive. Perhaps she'll get better, but I don't think so. For whatever reason, she believes with all her heart and mind that she is right in all that she does. It's justified to her because she wants it."

To be honest, she had no idea what to do. Prison would be hard on her, and for some reason, Kimber believed that she'd not live long there. Her rules, one sided as they were, would not go over well and the other inmates would have to retaliate, and that would get her killed. Long term health care would be no better either. She was set in her ways, and no one that had to work with her would be spared of her nastiness. Kimber sat down on the chair that was close to her and looked at Luke.

"I want her to be cared for, I do, but I don't think she'll appreciate it coming from me. No matter what we did for her, she'd find fault." Luke sat and told her that he agreed with her. "I'll never go and see her. As of the moment she told me that she killed my mother and lied to everyone, I washed my hands of her. I have to go to the trial, if there is one, but that will be the last time I see her. I have nothing to give her, nor do I want anything that she might ever try to give to me. I think...I honestly don't care what happens to her."

"I can work with that, honey." He opened his briefcase and handed her two sheets of paper. "These are copies of the same thing. Read them over. But what they say is that you absolve yourself of her care and anything to do with her. You're no longer responsible for her or any debt that she might incur, as well as anything that she might have done to you and Hannah in the past. By that I mean that you cannot sue her for what she might have taken from you. You're, as you say, washing your hands of her."

"You mean the stuff she did to me my whole life?" He nodded. "But does that mean she'll get away with the murders?"

"No. All this says is that you don't care what she does from now on, so long as you are not involved in it. You will have to come and testify about the notes that you took when talking to her. Not as her niece, but as a witness for the state." Kimber liked that and asked him for a pen. "You understand that the money that she took from you while you were in France is the only money that you're talking about?"

"What does that mean?" He grinned at her. "Why is it that each of you, and I mean Emersons and in-laws, each have that smile? Is it something that you get when you take on the last name? Because to me it says, the person that you're thinking about is so fucked right now."

"And you would be correct." He told her to sign her name as Kimber Emerson. Then when she did on both sheets of paper, he leaned back in his chair. "She has an account that has over eleven million dollars in it that belongs to you. Taken from your mother's accounts just after she was murdered. Your father, a man that I wish I could have met, had another account, but she's never been able to get into it. The only name on it is his. I've petitioned the courts to have that released to you as well. My advice—and you can do as you please—is to set that money aside for Hannah and any other children you might have. There is also the life insurance policy that belonged to your mother. And since she was murdered, the insured amount is doubled."

"How much are we talking?" He grinned again, and Kimber wanted to hit him. "I don't like you very much right now."

"Oh, but you're going to love me after I tell you. I promise." He handed her another set of papers. "With all your holdings and the offshore accounts, your net worth is just over seventy million. Not including your father's money, which I don't know the balance of as yet. Then there is the insurance money, the properties, as well as the now closed restaurants in both France and one in Georgia, where you apprenticed before going to France."

"That's not possible." Luke nodded and handed her the deeds. "I own two restaurants as well as homes...they seem to be all over the world. And she bitched about...well, everything."

"Pretty much. And if you want to rent them out, Jack and I would love to use the one you have in Florida. We'd like to go to the park down there and take Kelly." Luke stood up.

"I've taken the liberty of hiring you an attorney. I'm not in a position to help you overly much right now. You'll need someone that can work only with you, and someone you can trust. While you do have all this, some of it is in shambles. I'd go over it with Lee and see what you want to keep or sell. But my advice is, keep it for at least a year or two. You might change your mind about a few of them."

She was still sitting there when Hannah came and sat near her. Kimber pulled her into her arms and held her while Lee sat across from them. Handing him the paperwork that had been just given to her, she told him what Luke had said.

"He won't steer you wrong." She nodded. "Let's get some lunch and I'll tell you about the phone call I just got. Sloan also wants us to go to the restaurant site and look around. Apparently there are some things that they've unearthed that she wants you to see."

"Is it a dead body? Because right now, that would not surprise me." Hannah giggled. "I have a better idea. Let's go and have some lunch, get on a plane, and fly away from all this. I think I saw on that list that we have one...a plane, I mean. We could go to any number of those houses and live there like kings and never come back here."

"I have to go to school tomorrow." Hannah looked up at her. "I'm in sixth grade now. They said that I was smart."

"You are." Kimber looked at Lee. "So are you. I don't know what I would have done without you, Lee. I really don't."

"You would have muddled along until you came to the conclusion that someone was out there waiting for you and you had to find me." He laughed when she slapped his knee. "Lunch, restaurant, then home to do homework. I have to leave in a few days for California. There's a restaurant there that everyone is raving about that I must go and see to. As much as I would love for the two of you to come with me, Miss Hannah here needs to get her classes all worked on."

As they left the courthouse, the courtroom they had left was quiet. Neither of them mentioned it, and as they made their way out into the warm sunshine, Kimber thought of all the things she could do with the money. First and foremost, she was going to do just what Sloan had asked her to do about the large mansion her aunt had lived in.

The art community house was going to be great, and it would be something that her mom would have enjoyed too. Thinking about the name of the place, she decided to talk it over with Hannah and Lee.

Then there was the insurance money. Kimber was going to live for a very long time. Forever, she supposed. And when she'd talked to Lee last night, he said he was willing to have her change him as well. The thought of the two of them spending lifetimes together was scary, but also wonderful. The only thing that concerned her was Hannah. But they had time for that.

Cash and the rest of the family were in the diner when they arrived. Almost as soon as they walked in the door, they were greeted like they'd not just seen them an hour ago. Hugs were passed around like a basket of bread at dinner, and the kids were given small gifts, things that meant more to them than anything that they could have picked for themselves. As Kimber sat down, all the women, including Mabel, sat with her. She knew an ambush when she saw one.

"We'd like for you to cook for the next meeting of the minds. That's not what it's called. It's actually the Planner Committee for the town, but we meet every Monday." Sloan handed her a list of the members and she saw her name on it. Before she could ask her about it, Sloan continued. "We come up with things like the Christmas Ball, which will be here before we know it, as well as the Thanksgiving Parade. And we, of course, eat."

"All right." She laid the list down. "But I decide what we eat. I want to try some new things out, and this would be a good way to test them. If you're okay with that."

"Are you kidding? Guinea pigs for you? Hell yeah, I'm there." Jack laughed. "Besides, I think that we should have a family discount to this place. Do you have a name for it yet?"

"I do. It'll be called Emerson's. That's all." Jack grinned. "And before all that creative gunk that you have going on in your head goes spilling out, I want you to do me one thing. I want the advertising to be low key for a while, and the menu to be something that I can change daily without taking away from the style that you're going to give us."

"I can do that." Kimber wanted to make her swear, but she was afraid that she'd hit her. There was something about Jack that made Kimber think that she was a time bomb just waiting for someone to mess with her. And when they did, she was going to be all over them so that nothing was left to even identify. Addie giggled.

"She's harmless. Unless you piss her off. And that is yet to come." They all stared at Addie. "No, I'm not going to tell, but I would like to suggest one thing. That when she gets here, Graham's mate, we surround Graham like wagons in a war zone. He'll need us more than anyone has ever needed an Emerson until now."

"Graham? You meant his mate, right?" Addie shook her head at Sloan. "Is it bad? Will he be…is he going to be hurt?"

"Yes. Badly, too, if we don't protect him." Addie smiled. "You know that things can change, the outcome might be different? If we're there for him, he'll survive."

"We will be." Addie nodded at Sloan and looked at Kimber. The smile that she had on her face was soft and full of humor. Kimber asked her what was wrong.

"Your restaurant is going to be a huge success. Not only that, but you will be the talk of the town for years to come when you open."

"But no pressure, right?"

They all laughed, and Kimber tried not to think of what Addie meant. Her thoughts immediately went to her falling on her face, a flat out stupid move that would have them all laughing at her. When Addie put her hand on her arm, Kimber felt the fear go away and be replaced with calmness and well-being. Nodding, Kimber told her she was fine now. And she really was.

And with that, they ordered their food. Kimber looked around again. This was going to be the best thing that ever happened to her and her child, and she could not wait for it all to come together. The house, the restaurant, and the new committee she was on…Kimber was in heaven.

EMERSON WOLVES

NOW AVAILABLE

COMING SOON

Before You Go...

HELP AN AUTHOR

write a review

THANK YOU!

Share your voice and help guide other readers to these wonderful books. Even if it's only a line or two your reviews help readers discover the author's books so they can continue creating stories that you'll love. Login to your favorite retailer and leave a review. Thank you.

Kathi Barton, author of the bestselling series Force of Nature, lives in Nashport, Ohio with her husband Paul. In addition to writing full time Kathi likes to spend time with her eight grandkids, three children and three children-in-laws. She writes to relax and have fun.

Her muse, a cross between Jimmy Stewart and Hugh Jackman brings them to life for her readers in a way that has them coming back time and again for more. Her favorite genre is paranormal romance with a great deal of spice. You can visit Kathi on line and drop her an email if you'd like. She loves hearing from her fans. aaronskiss@gmail.com.

Follow Kathi on her blog: http://kathisbartonauthor.blogspot.com/